ST. PATRICK'S DAY ON ST. BARTS

THE HOLIDAY ADVENTURE CLUB BOOK TWO

STEPHANIE TAYLOR

1

MARCH 15

ST. BARTS, FRENCH WEST INDIES

It's not like Florida was an unpleasant, un-tropical place to be in mid-March. But as Lucy Landish walked through the lobby of the Hotel Christopher on St. Barts, she realized that there was tropical—as in pink and green decor; palm trees outside the grocery store; and fourteen swimming pools in every condominium community, and then there was *tropical*—as in views of an infinity pool that dropped off into a turquoise ocean; teak wood decks draped with women wearing expensive swimwear and diamonds; and a view of multi-million dollar yachts framed perfectly in the middle of a splay of palm fronds.

This island was one of a cluster in the Caribbean, a French West Indies outpost that had become a playground for the rich and famous, and just being there had already shifted Lucy's mood. Gone was the memory of the long and bumpy flight, and in its place was a balmy breeze blowing in through a wall of windows that had been completely pushed back to make the interior of the hotel feel as though it merged with the outdoors.

"So this is what vacation feels like, huh?" Nick Epperson strolled across the wide, polished wooden floors of the lobby, hands in his pockets as he turned his handsome face out toward the water.

"Haven't been on one in years, so I'd forgotten." He turned to give Lucy a half-smile as he nudged her arm with his elbow. "Thanks again for letting me tag along."

Lucy felt her heart do a little kick-flip in her chest, and not for the first time since she and Nick had embarked on this journey. Back on Amelia Island, Nick was her next door work neighbor, owner of a postal store called The Carrier Pigeon, and master of a completely charming black lab named Hemingway. He was also a slightly rumpled mystery novel writer who loved to tease her, and an incredibly thoughtful gift-giver who'd anonymously sent her a snow globe to mark her first trip abroad to Venice with the Holiday Adventure Club. To say her feelings about him were slightly more than friendly was an understatement, but their daily proximity back home kept them both on their best behavior.

Lucy smiled right back at him, breathing deeply as she closed her eyes and felt the warm breeze touch her skin. All around them, people flowed in and out of the hotel and settled on deck chairs that looked as though they'd come straight from the pages of *Architectural Digest* magazine.

The Holiday Adventure Club, Lucy thought, eyes still closed. She'd started this journey as something of a gift to herself on a personal level, and as a business venture that she hoped might kickstart her travel agency, but already she could feel that it was changing her. The plan was to hit a different location around the world for as many holidays as she could manage in the span of a year, and after spending Valentine's Day in Venice with a tour group that had signed up to join her, she was now perched on a tiny island in the Caribbean, ready to spend St. Patrick's Day on St. Barts with her sexy work neighbor and a bunch of people from places like Omaha, Ohio, and Ottawa. (Yes, truly with all the O places, and she had no idea why.)

"Let me get you a drink," Nick said, pulling one hand from the pocket of his navy blue shorts and holding it up to signal a passing staff member holding a silver tray of tropical-looking beverages.

Lucy opened her eyes and looked around again. St. Barts. She'd made this happen. There was something so satisfying in the moments when she was able to really appreciate the work that had gone into her move from Buffalo to Florida, the leap of faith it had taken to give up a career as a forensic pathologist and open her own business in a totally different field, and the growing sense of peace she felt with the ugly divorce she'd put behind her.

"Thanks, Nick," Lucy said, taking the tall, frosty glass from him and removing a wedge of pineapple from the lip of the drink. She took a bite of the tart fruit and smiled across the lobby at Alvin, the concierge she'd been in touch with over the past month as she'd planned this group excursion. "I'm so glad you're here," she said, bumping her shoulder against Nick's lightly. And she meant it; having him along was fun and exciting, and while she didn't want to mess up their work relationship at home, a part of her wasn't opposed to some vacation flirtation.

He smiled back at her. "Me too. I have to be honest with you, though: I really second-guessed taking this trip a few times." Nick flushed, looking surprisingly vulnerable.

Lucy put the hot pink straw to her lips and took a long pull of what turned out to be a piña colada. "Why?"

"Well," Nick said. "I didn't want to get in the way, you know?"

"You're not going to get in the way," Lucy said. "Come on, this is a vacation! All you need to do is relax and have a good time."

"But it's not just a vacation for you. You're here to work and to make your guests happy, and I just thought...you know. Me trying to take you out to dinner or snorkeling might mess up your other plans."

"You won't mess up my other plans. I *wanted* you to come," Lucy said, glancing around the lobby and taking in all of the chic, put-together women who seemed infinitely more put together than she felt. She mentally berated herself for sometimes feeling like a a thirteen-year-old masquerading in the body of a thirty-eight-year-old woman, but then plastered a convincingly confident smile on her face as Alvin approached them in his crisp, ironed shorts and polo shirt.

"Miss Landish," the young concierge said with a slight bow. "And sir," he said, turning slightly to give Nick a bow as well. "We are thrilled to have your group here this week, and I want to ensure that everything is comfortable for you and your guests. Is there anything I can do at this moment to improve your stay?" Alvin's French accent was smooth and charming.

"No, thank you, Alvin. So far everything is amazing."

There was nothing about the Hotel Christopher that Lucy would change, from the views, to the sumptuously elegant rooms and the relaxed, tropical vibe. It was all better than she'd even dreamed it might be.

Alvin bowed once more and left them to stare at the water. From hidden speakers wafted a blend of jazz, French music, and mellow steel drums.

"When is everyone arriving?" Nick asked, leading her out through the open wall of windows and out onto the wooden planks that surrounded the infinity pool. There were deck chairs covered in muted shades of gray, and each had a precisely placed neck roll that was wrapped in smooth orange canvas. People lounged around, talking and laughing as they sipped drinks and massaged their skin with tanning oils and lotions that made their bodies glisten in the sun.

Lucy picked two chairs facing the edge of the pool so they could gaze out at the water beyond. "Tomorrow," she said, taking a small sip of her slushy piña colada to keep the brain freeze at bay. "Guests start showing up in the morning, and then we'll have a group dinner at seven."

To his credit, Nick's eyes stayed focused on the drink in his hand as a trio of incredibly gorgeous, lithe women in bikini bottoms that looked as if they'd been intentionally wedged between their firm, undimpled cheeks passed by. Lucy knew that she and Nick were nothing but friends on this trip, but his care not to get caught ogling other women struck her as gentlemanly. Once the women had fully passed, he looked in Lucy's direction.

"Right on," he said, lifting his drink and taking a sip. "I could sit here and watch the water until tomorrow, as long as someone kept delivering piña coladas on a regular schedule."

Lucy reached over and slapped Nick's thigh. "No sir!" she said, crossing her feet at the ankles as she leaned back in the surprisingly comfortable deck chair. "We have work to do before the guests get here."

Nick leaned back in his own chair and set his drink on the small table between them. The sky was a soft blue, the sun mellow and warm. He squinted in Lucy's direction.

"Yeah," Nick said, holding up a hand to shield his eyes as he watched Lucy close hers. "You don't look like someone who's about to bolt up and get any work done."

"I am, Epperson," she said, sounding fake-annoyed as she waved a hand dismissively. "I definitely am. Just as soon as I take a tiny cat nap here in the sun." Lucy opened one eye and smiled at Nick. "Hey," she said, patting his leg again. "Thanks for coming along. I mean it."

Nick picked up his drink and turned his face up to the sun. "Well, it was a big sacrifice on my part. But you're welcome."

They laughed and then proceeded to do absolutely nothing for the next two hours.

2

MARCH 16
SOMEWHERE OVER THE ATLANTIC

Finn Barlow pushed at the carry-on bag he'd shoved under the seat in front of him. At six-foot-two, he needed more legroom than even First Class could offer, but on the budget of a firefighter from a small coastal California town, he was jammed into Coach. At least he had a window.

"Not much space for a tall drink of water like yourself, is there, Captain?" A woman who had to be sixty-five if she was a day leaned across the empty middle seat and filled Finn's nostrils with the over-powering smell of liberally-applied perfume.

Finn's mouth quirked into a smile as he glanced down to double-check whether or not he'd accidentally put on his Whitefish Fire Department softball team jersey, or if he'd somehow dressed in a way that made him look like a Federal Air Marshal or something.

"You can tell I'm a firefighter?" he finally asked, not finding anything about how he was dressed that might give him away.

The woman leaned back in her seat with a satisfied smile. "Well," she said, letting her eyes flick over his hard chest and smooth face. "I figured either ex-military, firefighter, or cop. Lucky guess."

With a laugh, Finn rubbed one hand over the knee of his olive green cargo pants. "Okay, I'll give you that. There are tells, right?" He ran one hand over his short hair. "Similar haircuts. Orderly appearance."

"Oh honey," the woman said, tapping bright red nails on the armrest between the seats. "It's more than that." She sat up straighter, wiggling her shoulders as she spoke. "It's the way you carry yourself. Your posture. Your physique. The way you wear a watch," she said, nodding at his wrist, where a heavy-looking digital watch sat squarely against his tanned skin. "There's a precision to your clothes. To the way you tie your shoes."

Finn lifted up a foot—at least as much as he could in the tight space—and looked at the way his laces lay flat against his shoe, the bow made out of two identical lengths of lace.

"See?" the woman said, watching Finn as he inspected himself. "It's not just one thing, it's all the things. And they're all very *sexy* things," she added, dropping her voice.

Finn's head snapped up in surprise. This woman was nearly old enough to be his grandmother. *Is there something about me that sends off come-hither vibes to women twice my age?* he wondered.

"Elise," the woman said, offering him a soft hand. Finn stared at it for a fraction of a second before taking it in his own and giving it a gentle shake. There was no way he wanted to crush the fingers of a senior citizen on a flight to paradise. "I'm headed to St. Barts for the regatta. I want to find a rich man—a sugar daddy, if you will."

Finn called on every fiber of his being to hold in the laugh that wanted to escape. If a sixty-five-year-old woman was looking for a sugar daddy, she'd need to find a man well into his eighties or nineties to fit the bill. *Yikes*, Finn thought. *But at least I'm safe. Okay, I'm safe-ish*, he corrected his train of thought, watching as Elise kept his hand in hers for several seconds more than was necessary.

"Finn," he said, giving her hand a final squeeze and then slipping his fingers from hers.

"Captain Finn," Elise said. She breathed in slowly and then released it, looking out into the distance dreamily like a woman who was trying on a fantasy of herself married to a young fireman.

This woman was a real ticket. Finn felt nothing but amusement as he watched her uncross and recross her legs in the small space. She turned her body so that it was angled in his direction in spite of the seat belt holding her in place.

"So you're going to find a date at the regatta?" Finn asked politely, wishing they were already in the air and that the drink cart was nearby.

Elise laughed, a tinkling sound like a shrimp fork touching the rim of a champagne glass. Her pants were made of a royal blue satin, and her blouse was a colorful splash pattern with oversized pearl buttons. She reminded Finn a bit of the character Blanche Devereaux from his mom's all-time favorite tv show, *The Golden Girls*.

"Not a date, sweetie," Elise said, straightening the leg of her pants by giving the fabric a gentle tug. She swung one high-heeled foot around loosely as she talked, dangling the shoe from her toes as her heel slid out. There was no question in Finn's mind that Elise would be a real catch for some divorced guy in a toupee, a man she would undoubtedly find in the hotel bar. "I definitely don't need any more dates. I need a *man*. One who can afford me," she said, pressing her lips together in a surprisingly practical way. The sexy ingenue act fell away as she slipped her foot fully into her shoe and uncrossed her legs. "I don't have time to mess around."

"Oh," Finn said, for lack of any better response.

Elise caught herself and loosened up, leaning toward Finn confidentially once again. She put a hand on his forearm and spoke in a near whisper. "Look, Captain Finn," she said, drawing in a breath. "I know we're not even wheels-up on this journey yet, but you've got an honest face. You're clearly a man of some distinction and integrity, so I'm going to be completely straightforward with you: I find myself in a pickle that love alone won't undo," Elise paused, putting both hands in the air as if in surrender, "It's also gonna take some money."

Finn blinked a few times. "I hear you." Of course, at his age and in his present predicament, there was nothing he could imagine that love alone *wouldn't* undo, but he wanted to try to see her perspective.

"Well, life has a way of turning you on your ear sometimes." Elise shifted her body forward to face the seat in front of her, gripping both armrests in her hands. "But fortunately I found this trip online with a group called 'The Holiday Adventure Club'—"

"Wait, you're headed to St. Barts with the same group I am," Finn said, frowning. When he'd read about the trip, he'd assumed that the word "adventure" in the title might indicate a more youthful, water-fall-hiking, rope bridge-walking, zipline-cruising clientele than the woman seated to his left.

Elise smiled at him, her bright red lips pulling into a happy grin. "Well, I'll be damned!" she said.

As they talked, the plane taxied and took off and Finn relaxed and accepted the fact that Elise most definitely planned to talk to him throughout the duration of the flight. In short order, he learned that she was indeed over sixty (though she refused to say more than that), and that her first husband, Douglas Rittenhour, had passed away of a heart attack nearly twenty years ago. Elise was an executive assistant by trade, but fancied herself a bit of a gourmet chef slash ballroom dancer slash community activist. As she talked and laughed, she frequently leaned across the middle seat to touch Finn's arm playfully.

When it was his turn to share, Finn told Elise about his first few years on the job with the fire department in Whitefish. He talked about how both his father and grandfather had been firemen, and the fact that he'd be turning thirty in a few months. Finn told her that he loved laying on his back and listening to someone read books aloud to him in his small cabin (his most recent favorite had been *The Heart's Invisible Furies*, though he let Elise believe that it had been read aloud by some faceless narrator via audiobook, and not by a half-naked woman next to him in bed), and that he never ate sushi, but couldn't get enough of his mom's shepherd's pie. Finn admitted that he lived in fear of being called to the scene of a crime or an accident where someone he knew had been badly hurt (an eventuality, given that he'd been born and raised in Whitefish and knew practically everyone), and that if his parents had asked him what he'd *really* wanted to do with his life, he probably would have chosen to go to college on the East coast and study literature.

As the plane banked and the captain let them know that they were beginning their approach to the Sint Maarten airport, Elise straightened her blouse and secured her tray table.

"You know, Captain Finn," she said, casting him a sideways glance as he sat his seat upright and shoved at the bag under the seat in front of him again. "I feel like I already know you like a real friend."

Finn smiled at her; they'd just talked for the entire three-hour flight from Miami. "Well, you know about as much about me as my friends do. But I do feel obligated to point out that I'm definitely *not* a captain—yet. I'm just a lowly firefighter."

"Ain't nothing lowly about fighting fires, doll," Elise said with a wink. "But you know what I don't know, Captain?"

"What's that?" Finn lifted an eyebrow; he was pretty sure there was nothing he hadn't covered as they'd raced through the sky toward their destination.

Elise leaned close again. "I don't know why you're going on a trip to St. Barts with the Holiday Adventure Club and not with a gorgeous broad who's got a suitcase full of bikinis and a libido like a racehorse."

Finn swallowed hard before answering. "I'm on this journey alone," he said, finding the words difficult to spit out, "to get over a woman, not to find one."

"Ah, young love gone wrong," Elise said knowingly, patting his arm as the plane began to descend in earnest.

Finn was tempted to correct her, but instead he gave her a close-lipped smile. And it *was* true that at least one of them had been young, but the person who comprised the other half of the doomed romance was only about fifteen years younger than Elise, a fact that he didn't particularly feel like disclosing at the moment.

"Yeah," he said instead, leaning his head back against the seat. "Sometimes it just doesn't work out, you know?"

Elise made a *tsk-tsk* sound as if she were personally disappointed in any girl who'd let Finn get away. He let her hold his hand all the way to their gate at the airport.

3

MARCH 16

ST. BARTS

"Roster of guests joining us?" Lucy asked, looking at the list in her hand as she sat on the balcony of her hotel room.

"Check," Nick responded.

"Dinner reservations confirmed for twenty-two people at seven-thirty?"

"Check."

"List of our people who've checked into the hotel so far?"

"Got it."

Lucy looked up at Nick; he was smirking.

"You ever give any thought to being a drill sergeant?" Nick joked.

"The only way I'm even close to being orderly and precise enough for the military is from my years standing in front of an autopsy table," Lucy said. "There is a definite order and a necessary precision to that job, so I guess I bring that with me." She held out a hand and Nick passed her the list of every Holiday Adventure Clubber joining them on St. Barts, along with a second list of people who'd already checked into the Hotel Christopher.

It was lunch time on the day of the guests' arrival, and Lucy had tossed and turned all night, thinking of last minute things she needed to do. Granted, the hotel itself was so sumptuous and well-appointed that the guests would undoubtedly arrive, check in, and instantly be wowed by the views and the luxury, but Lucy really wanted them to feel welcomed and cared for by the leader of their travel group.

"You're just really thorough," Nick said, shoving his hands into the pockets of his shorts as he stood and looked out at the water. In contrast to Lucy's tired eyes, messy bun, and wrinkled sundress, Nick looked well-rested, relaxed, and dressed for adventure.

Lucy sighed. "Well, you know how it is," she said, following his gaze. "I've got a lot to prove. I chose a new career path that's foreign to me, so I feel like every step of the way requires me to check and double-check my own work. But again, that's also a habit gleaned from my old job."

Nick pulled out the chair opposite hers at the little patio table and sat down. He leaned forward, resting his elbows on his knees as he looked at her intently. "Listen, you really don't have anything to prove. You're killing this whole thing, and you're only on trip number two of the entire year."

Lucy gave a laugh that sounded more like a huff. "I don't know about *killing it*."

"Come on, Dr. Landish," Nick said gruffly. "I can tell you didn't sleep because you look like something Hemingway dragged in from the backyard, but give yourself some credit here."

That actually made Lucy laugh out loud—a big, hearty guffaw. "I look like something your dog dragged in from outside? Dear god..." She put a hand into the frizz of her auburn hair and looked down self-consciously at her rumpled clothes. "The way I look is entirely incongruous with being called 'doctor,' you know? And it feels amazing being told that I look like roadkill."

"Hey, it's nothing a shower and some coffee won't fix," Nick assured her. "But seriously. I'm super impressed with this whole operation and the trip is barely starting."

Lucy pondered this. Her divorce, her mother's growing list of medical needs, and the sting of betrayal by her ex-boyfriend, Charlie, had certainly done a number on her head. Sometimes Lucy wondered why she'd even dated a guy with so little appeal, but it was easy to chalk it up now to loneliness during her first months on Amelia Island when she hadn't really known anyone. Things had ultimately ended between her and Charlie when she'd caught him in a compromising position with her roommate, a girl he was now squiring around Amelia Island like she was Princess Di and not a girl named Katrina from Georgia with dubious taste in men. So good riddance to the both of them.

"I hear you, Nick." Lucy looked up and into his handsome face. She wanted to internalize his compliments about her work and not brush them off. Building confidence in a new venture happened one brick at a time, and she could use all the bricks he was offering.

Not only was Nick her next-door work neighbor, but he was also her friend, cheerleader, and confidante. He'd walked her through the Charlie aftermath with the kind of patience usually reserved for female friends during evenings of cocktails and drunken tears. "And thank you. For always listening, and being encouraging," she said.

Nick slapped the glass table top and stood up again. "Good. We've got that settled. Now get your butt in the shower and meet me in the lobby in thirty minutes. I'll order us coffee and breakfast and we can go over the list of activities and people at least a hundred more times if you want. I'm here as your lowly assistant or to help in whatever capacity you need me to."

Lucy stood up and followed Nick through the suite, picking up a pillow from the messy bed and tossing it at him jokingly. It hit his shoulder and he ducked as if he'd been hit by shrapnel. "I'm under attack!" he shouted, lunging for the door.

Lucy watched with a smile as he walked down the hall.

"Thirty minutes, Landish! That's all you've got!" Nick punched the elevator button and stepped into the car as the doors slid open.

She stood there in the quiet hallway for a moment, her bare feet sinking into the plush carpet. *St. Barts*, she thought to herself. *I made it to St. Barts.* It was just a quiet moment of reflection, but one she needed to re-set and get ready for the coming week.

With a tired smile, Lucy closed the door and went to take a hot shower.

LUCY ENTERED THE LOBBY AT SIX-THIRTY AFTER SPENDING THE LION'S share of the day with Nick. They'd had breakfast and coffee, then taken a tour around the island in the little blue rental jeep that looked like a cross between a golf cart and a Mini Cooper, gathering as much intel as possible to share with the guests over dinner.

As she walked across the lobby now, low-heeled sandals clicking against the marble floors, Lucy was confronted by a vampy senior citizen with bottle-red hair and nails to match. Her creamy skin was cinched into a corset-like emerald green dress, and she held a microphone in one hand. The woman stood next to a glossy black piano, conferring with the pianist.

"Good evening," she finally said into the mic. Her voice carried through the lobby with its dimmed lights and hushed coolness. A small crowd of people in khaki shorts, collared shirts, sundresses, and slacks with loafers sat on overstuffed couches and chairs, faces turned expectantly in her direction. "I'm Elise Rittenhour, and I've recently arrived here on St. Barts like the rest of you," she purred, holding the microphone away from her mouth just enough that her voice floated sweetly around the room.

Lucy stopped in her tracks. Elise Rittenhour. She knew that name. Elise was scheduled to be a part of her group. A feeling of dread swept over Lucy, followed quickly by a cold sweat. Somehow one of her guests had beat her to the punch and was holding court before she'd even gotten the chance to say hello to the other travelers.

"I'm just a lonely widow from Ft. Worth, Texas, here on this trip with the Holiday Adventure Club. I'm hoping for a little relaxation in paradise, and I'm sure you are too," Elise said. She turned a bright smile on everyone in her line of vision as she glanced around the lobby. "And if I find romance along the way, then so be it." With a quick nod of her coiffed red head, she let the pianist know that it was time to start.

Elise launched right into "At Last" by Etta James, giving a throaty, emotional rendition that kept all eyes on her.

"What in the hell..." Lucy stood next to a huge round table in the center of the lobby, partially hiding behind an oversized vase of orchids and hibiscus that gave a pop of vibrant color to the otherwise neutral decor. She was stuck: she couldn't turn heel and head back to the elevators, nor could she interrupt Elise's unplanned performance without looking like a total jerk.

As she watched, feeling upstaged, Nick sidled up to Lucy and positioned himself just behind her right shoulder. "Is she your opening act?"

Lucy shook her head, but she was speechless. Instead of saying anything, she waited for Elise to finish singing, then took a deep breath and strode up to the microphone, holding out a hand as a round of applause punctuated by a few whistles gave way to some chatter as people commented on Elise's performance.

"Hi," Lucy said, stepping into the spot that Elise had just vacated. She glanced at the older woman's hourglass figure as she stepped away from the microphone, waving both hands at the crowd like Marilyn Monroe leaving the stage after belting out "Happy Birthday, Mr. President."

"Hello," Lucy started again, aiming for a smile this time as she took in the mostly middle-aged faces of the people gathered around her. "I'm Lucy Landish, trip organizer at the Holiday Adventure Club, and—as you all know—that was Elise Rittenhour." Lucy wasn't sure what else to say about Elise, so she waited as another round of polite, subdued applause worked its way through the crowd. "Anyhow, welcome to St. Barts. I'm thrilled to see all of you, and I'm very much looking forward to getting to know you as we explore the island together. Of course I'm here to help out in any way I can as you make plans and enjoy this gorgeous slice of paradise." She glanced over at the table where she'd just been standing and noticed Nick leaning against it, arms folded as he watched her with a smile. "And this," she said, holding out a hand in Nick's direction, "is Nick Epperson, my right hand man. If you can't find me, just ask him for anything you need and we'll get it worked out as fast as we can. Now, let's head out to dinner, shall we?"

Lucy set the microphone back on its stand and stepped gingerly over the cord that snaked in front of her.

"Darling," Elise Rittenhour said, holding out both hands to take Lucy's in hers. "I hope my little impromptu performance didn't step on your toes." She looked chagrined, but only mildly so. "I just love a good audience, you know?"

"Mrs. Rittenhour," Lucy said, squeezing Elise's hands and digging deep to find a well of fortitude while dealing with the kind of bold, attention-hoarding older woman she knew could overpower the entire trip, given the opportunity. "That was quite a performance."

Elise put one hand to her chest modestly, as if accepting a heartfelt compliment. "Oh, honey," she said. "Thank you."

"I'm thrilled to finally meet you in person," Lucy went on. "And I hope this trip is everything you dreamed it would be."

"I have some high expectations for this vacation," Elise admitted. "And I want to tell you all about them, but first I'd love to introduce you to my nearest and dearest friend on this entire island."

Lucy frowned; she could have sworn that Elise Rittenhour had signed up for the trip as a solo traveler.

"This," Elise said, waving at a young, fresh-faced man in cargo shorts and a sky blue polo shirt, "is Captain Finn." She stepped aside as the man approached, his cheeks and skin pink and dewy like he'd just stepped out of a hot shower, which he clearly had, judging by the damp hair.

"Finn Barlow," he said, holding out a hand.

Finn Barlow—another familiar name.

"Lucy Landish. It's a pleasure to meet you." She shook Finn's hand, trying to puzzle out how brassy Elise and this young, muscular guy knew one another. If memory served, Mr. Barlow was from the west coast, and Elise had just told the crowd she was from Texas. Grandmother and beloved grandson, perhaps?

"You look confused, darling," Elise butted in, "so I'll just tell you: Captain Finn and I were seat mates on the flight from Miami, and we became bosom buddies in no time." She smiled, looking pleased with herself. "But I have to clarify: we did *not* join the Mile High Club together, though not for my lack of trying." Elise laughed wickedly, clapping her hands together.

Finn's eyes went wide, and his pink post-shower skin deepened into a mortified shade of red.

"Well," Lucy said, trying to pull together an appropriate response. "I can barely pry myself out of my seat to use the bathroom during a flight, so I admire anyone who even considers those kind of mid-air acrobatics in the loo."

From the way Finn's eyes closed for an extra-long blink, Lucy could tell that *this* wasn't necessarily the response he'd been hoping for.

But Elise howled with laughter and reached over to Lucy, patting her cheek. "You're a doll," she said, letting her eyes trail after a distinguished, gray-haired man in an expensive dinner jacket and butter-soft Gucci loafers. "Will you two excuse me?" Elise said, not waiting for an answer before squaring her shoulders, popping a hip, and then following the man with her backside swaying alluringly as he made his way to the piano.

"I just..." Finn started, closing his eyes, squinting, and tilting his head all at once like he was trying to squelch some sort of physical pain. "Wow. So yeah."

Lucy laughed. "Sorry, I shouldn't have encouraged her."

"I don't think she needs much encouragement," Finn said. "I've only known the woman for a handful of hours, but I think I can safely say that Elise has the kind of self-confidence that starts wars and fuels rap battles and dance-offs."

"Rap battles and dance-offs?" Lucy's eyes crinkled with laughter.

"Seriously," Finn said. "If you're not Eminem, then you need some major *cajones* to get up on stage for a rap battle. And I think Elise has the stones for it."

Lucy tried to center herself. "I feel like this whole trip just got off to a completely unexpected start," she said, waving a hand like she could erase the past ten minutes. "But I'm happy you're with us, Finn. I'm also curious about why Elise keeps calling you Captain Finn."

"I'm a firefighter, but not a captain," he said, nodding as his eyes skimmed the lobby and landed on Elise, who was gazing up at the man in the Gucci loafers with a look of open admiration as she stood about six inches too close to him. "Which I figure means that at some point Elise will make a totally off-color joke about my giant hose or how she'd like to slide down my pole. I'm just waiting for it."

Lucy couldn't hold back her laughter this time. "She's a real character—at least from what I've seen so far."

"Yeah." Finn nodded. "What you've seen so far is a great introduction to Elise Rittenhour."

"Hey." Nick walked up to them, looking at Finn with a guarded smile. "So we're off to the races, huh?"

"It appears that we are." Lucy looked at Nick and then back at Finn. "Nick Epperson, this is Finn Barlow, Finn, this is Nick, one of my close friends from Florida. He was ready to get out of town, so he joined me on this trip."

Finn and Nick shook hands, but Lucy could feel Nick tense up beside her even as Finn's face remained open and friendly.

"So, I guess we should get everyone loaded into the chartered vans out front," Lucy said, resting her hand in the crook of Nick's arm. "Finn, maybe you want to grab your lady friend and see if she's still planning on coming with us?" Lucy nodded at Elise, who was laughing uproariously at something the silver fox in the Gucci loafers had said. Seemingly from nowhere, a champagne flute had materialized in Elise's hand.

"I'll check with her and meet you guys out front." Finn backed away with a small salute.

"Nice guy," Nick said gruffly. "But is that older lady really his girlfriend?"

"Oh god no, I was teasing him," Lucy said, matching her steps to Nick's as they headed across the lobby to the sliding doors that led out onto the gorgeously manicured grounds out front. "Apparently they met on the airplane and Elise is quite a flirt."

Nick glanced back over his shoulder with a look of admiration. "Alright," he said as he watched Elise. "I see you, girl. Get after it, you randy cougar."

"Nick!" Lucy slapped his arm as they stepped through the open doors and onto the top step that led to the parking area where the vans were waiting. A rushing manmade waterfall spilled over the rock formation in front of the hotel. "She's a slightly sexy grandma, not a salivating beast."

"She's a saucy minx, is what she is," Nick clarified. "And you better watch out for me, because I'm right in her wheelhouse, baby. I could get eaten, if I'm not careful." Nick made a playful growl and held up his hands like they were claws.

Lucy stood on the step in front of the hotel, hands on both hips as she looked at Nick with mock astonishment. "You know, as punishment for putting that image in my head, I should let you fend for yourself on this one," she said, holding up a hand and waving for the vans to pull up.

Nick smirked. "I can handle a firecracker like Elise. Just watch me."

Lucy rolled her eyes and reached for the door of the first van, sliding it open and then turning to the knot of guests waiting to be ferried to dinner. "Step right up," she said with a huge smile. "Get yourself situated and then we'll be off to dinner here shortly at the famed Casa with its gorgeous view of the harbor as the sun sets."

People took Lucy's hand each time she offered it, stepping up into the rented van and buckling themselves in as she greeted each of them warmly and tried to commit names and faces to memory. Within minutes, the three vans were loaded and Lucy climbed in last, but not before she spotted Nick seated in the van ahead of hers on a bench seat next to Elise Rittenhour. She chuckled to herself and shook her head.

"We're headed to Casa," she said to the driver, patting the back of his seat before sitting back and inhaling the first deep breath she'd taken all day.

❦

THE TABLES AT THE RESTAURANT WERE PUSHED UP AGAINST THE OPEN windows that looked out over the harbor. Servers in crisp white aprons waited for the large Holiday Adventure Club group to arrive, hands clasped behind their backs, smiles on their faces.

Lucy led everyone into the dining room and they scattered themselves around the long, family-style table, *oohing* and *aahing* at the masts and colorful flags of the yachts docked in the harbor nearby. Palm trees swayed against the evening sky and a light breeze blew over the table as the ladies opened napkins and rested them across their laps.

As the last person to take a seat, Lucy realized that she'd missed her chance to sit with a guest she hadn't spoken to yet, or to sit near Nick or even next to Finn, who seemed funny and interesting, and instead she pulled out the only available seat and sat down next to Elise Rittenhour with a quiet sigh.

"Darling," Elise said, reaching for a water glass. Her lacquered nails clicked against the sweaty goblet as she picked it up. "I'm so glad to be sitting with you."

"Likewise," Lucy said, lifting the printed menu that rested on the center of her bread plate. She perused the entrees: lobster, grilled prawns, fresh fruit and vegetables, a side of caviar, homemade mashed potatoes. It all sounded delicious.

"That friend of yours from Florida looks like a college professor— the kind all the girls stay after class so they can pretend to ask him extra questions," Elise said, leaning over and bumping Lucy with her shoulder like they were two girlfriends gossiping over a bottle of wine.

"He does look a little like that, doesn't he? But Nick is actually an author. He writes mystery novels." Lucy frowned. "Although I'm not quite sure what he's working on now."

"Honey," Elise said, straightening her flatware so that it lined up precisely next to her empty plate. "If he's here, then I'd say he's working on *you*."

Lucy choked on a sip of water.

A waiter swooped in then with an open bottle of wine, holding it up to offer Lucy and Elise a glass. They both accepted.

"Now, tell me more about you," Lucy said, clearing her throat and changing the subject smoothly as she swirled the wine around in her glass and took a fragrant sip. "You're from Texas, and obviously you're a natural performer."

"Well, sweetheart, I hate to burst your bubble about aging, but nothing about this operation is *completely* natural," Elise said with a wink, waving a hand over her full bosom and smoothly plumped cheeks and lips. "I work hard for this."

"Hey, you've got to suffer for beauty, right? My grandmother used to tell me as she yanked a brush through my tangled hair." Lucy smiled at the memory. It had hurt, but it had also been a valuable lesson.

"At your age, there's still no suffering, Lucy. Enjoy that." Elise set her wineglass on the table and leaned back, eyes focused on the multi-million dollar yachts in the harbor. "As for me, yes, I'm from Texas. Widowed for longer than I care to admit, and looking for a gentleman on this trip. Someone I can count on."

Lucy thought about this. "I'm sorry to hear about your husband."

"Oh, don't you worry about that. I'm okay," Elise assured her, reaching over and taking Lucy's right hand in her left one and giving it a squeeze.

A bird landed on the ledge of the open window, turning one eye toward the table and watching for a moment as people laughed and drank wine before it lifted its white body and flew away again on strong wings.

"I guess I'm curious about what you mean when you say you want someone you can count on," Lucy said carefully, hoping to find out more about Elise, a woman who had sung to a crowd of complete strangers and then followed a man across the lobby to try to pick-pocket his room key as they sipped expensive champagne.

Elise's eyes narrowed. "It gets hard being alone," she said quietly. "Lonely. Doing it all on your own as a woman can be empowering, Lucy, but it can also be exhausting. I want to wake up to someone. To fall asleep with someone. To not have those moments that we single gals have where we start mentally calculating and doing the math: *Can I afford this? Who will pay for that? How long can I live on the amount of money I've got socked away?* You know what I mean?" She turned to look Lucy in the eye. "Sometimes you just want somebody you can count on."

Her words hit Lucy like a punch to the gut. "Yeah," she said, nodding and looking into her wineglass as the candlelight on their table flickered and glinted. "I do know what you mean."

At the opposite end of the table, Nick was sitting between two jolly looking women with pink cheeks and carefully curled and styled hair. Lucy knew from the quick introductions in the van on the way over that this matronly duo was Elaine Darwin and Maribel Truman from Idaho, sisters who had wanted to take a trip together to celebrate Elaine's sixtieth birthday and Maribel's third divorce. Maribel had one arm draped across the back of Nick's chair as she leaned across him to say something to her sister. As the women broke out in a shared laugh, Nick looked up and caught Lucy's eye. He winked.

Finn Barlow had been taken in by a married couple from New Mexico, and from where Lucy sat, she could see that the husband was regaling him with a story of some sort that most likely involved a giant fish, as he was using both hands to mime reeling in a big one.

Lucy looked around the table: everyone seemed to be engaged in various conversations, talking and eating bread and butter to soak up the wine that was already flowing. Even Elise had turned to the man on the other side of her and was chatting him up animatedly while his wife was in the restroom. This moment of respite gave Lucy the chance to sip her wine and think about the rest of the year ahead. Venice had been an amazing and wild start to this string of travel adventures, and on that trip she'd made two new friends, Carmen and Bree, and proved to herself that she *could* pick a destination and just go there. It had been scary, liberating, nerve-wracking, and ultimately satisfying.

But now St. Barts. The servers came around and set down

gorgeous presentations of pasta with truffle, and risotto with spiny lobster. Some of the plates were decorated with edible flowers and grilled vegetables that looked so bright and vibrant that Lucy wondered if the restaurant had a garden out back to grow their own produce. Her stomach growled and she realized that she hadn't actually eaten a bite of anything since she and Nick had sat down to coffee and breakfast that morning.

As she tucked into her own plate of fois gras with fresh figs, Lucy tried to tamp down the feeling of deep exhaustion that settled over her. The sky had turned a deep amethyst over the harbor, and the yachts were lit up like Christmas trees. Jazz music came from speakers all around the restaurant, and next to her, Elise howled at a story that someone across the table was telling.

It was a moment of pure contentment for Lucy. She was more than a thousand miles from home, enjoying a world-class dinner with a bunch of friendly, happy strangers. Her mother hadn't texted or called with anything urgent or disastrous in the past three days, and she was about to tour the island and take part in all the amenities that St. Barts had to offer.

Lucy put a bite of rich, buttery fois gras in her mouth and chewed thoughtfully. She really should be feeling more excited, even with the fatigue that came with travel and hard work.

And yet...and yet.

Something was nagging at her. Had she forgotten to do anything before leaving home? No, her neighbor had agreed to feed her cat, Joji, and she'd left plenty of food for him. Had she left her flat iron plugged in? No, it wasn't that. Lucy looked around the table again as she speared a fig with her fork.

With the bite halfway to her mouth, she realized what it was: it was something Elise had said. *I want to wake up to someone. To fall asleep with someone. Sometimes you just want somebody you can count on.* Once upon a time she'd had that. And when it had been good, it had been very, very good. Being married was something she still believed in, even if it hadn't worked out so well the first time.

Lucy reached for her wineglass. Sipped. Sipped again. Felt the unwelcome sensation of tears prickling at the back of her eyes without warning. She blinked them away and smiled at Elaine Darwin at the other end of the table.

But the tears still threatened to fall, because she realized that it was completely true: sometimes you *did* just want somebody you could count on.

4

MARCH 17

ST. BARTS

"Happy St. Patrick's Day!" Lucy called out, waving at Elaine and Maribel as they drank their coffee by the pool the next morning. She'd woken up feeling far less pensive and completely ready to start sending her fellow travelers out to explore the island.

"You're looking festive." Finn Barlow strolled over to where Lucy stood, white ceramic coffee cup in one hand, the other tucked into the pocket of his shorts as he eyed her shamrock green linen romper. She knew that the shorts showed off her Florida tan and the wedge-heeled espadrilles made her legs look long and lean, and the solid night of sleep she'd just gotten had perked her up considerably.

With a note of playful confidence, Lucy tilted her head to one side, glanced at his khaki shorts and navy blue t-shirt, and said: "And you're looking like a man who forgot to wear green and is hoping to get pinched."

Finn laughed loudly. "You got me there, Lucy. Are you offering to pinch me, or should I give Elise first dibs?"

Lucy tucked her clipboard under one arm as she reached out and took the cup of coffee that Alvin the concierge had kindly procured for her. "Thanks, Alvin," she said. He gave a single nod and left wordlessly. "Well," Lucy said, turning back to Finn. "I'd never want to dip my toe in another woman's pond, so I'd better let her do it."

Finn made an *aw, shucks* face and snapped his fingers. "Fair enough. Now, what's the plan for today? I'd really like to know more about the regatta."

Lucy started walking, holding her coffee carefully as she made her way to a lounge chair by the pool. Finn sat in the chair next to hers.

"The regatta is definitely an exciting part of being here during the month of March." Lucy crossed her legs at the knee and she noticed that Finn glanced at her thighs as she did. She couldn't pretend it wasn't flattering. "The 'Bucketeers,' as the sailors are called, are all arriving here on the island as we speak, and the race officially starts tomorrow and lasts for three days."

"Why are they called Bucketeers?" Finn planted his feet on the pavement and sipped his coffee as he watched Lucy's face. Even first thing in the morning he looked well-rested and fresh-faced, a natural side effect of being under thirty, Lucy thought with mild envy.

"The regatta is actually called the 'Bucket Regatta,' hence the cute name for the racers."

"Ah. Got it."

"There are only thirty super-yachts in the race, and it's by invitation only, so basically only the best sailors in the world participate. It's one of the most impressive nautical events of the year."

"So people with money," Finn said knowingly, looking at her over the rim of his mug.

"People with *a lot* of money," Lucy agreed. She glanced up as two men who looked as if they'd just stepped off a Ralph Lauren runway walked past. Both wore sweaters knotted around their broad shoulders, had hair that looked as if they'd paid two hundred dollars apiece to have winged angels run their delicate fingers from roots to ends, and wore watches that Lucy didn't need to see up close to peg as Rolexes.

Finn nodded in their direction. "Bucketeers, maybe?"

Lucy gave a one-shoulder shrug. "Could be."

"Elise is missing out," Finn said, looking around the pool deck. "I think those are the kind of guys she's looking for."

Lucy had a response to that, but just as she was about to speak, her Apple watch buzzed and she glanced down at it: it was her mother. Maybe thinking about her the night before at dinner had summoned her, or maybe Lucy was just due for a mini-crisis. She breathed in slowly, then exhaled intentionally for a count of four.

"I'm sorry, Finn. I need to take this call," Lucy said, setting her coffee on the little table between their chairs and reaching for her phone, which she'd set on top of her clipboard. "I'll be right back."

Lucy walked around the far edge of the pool, stopping next to a palm tree to look out at the blue water in the distance.

"Hi, Mom," she said, trying to keep the note of resignation from her voice as she slipped her free hand into the pocket of her shorts and kicked the base of the palm tree lightly with one foot.

"How long will you be gone this time?" No greeting. Her mother's voice was crisp and impatient.

"I'm in St. Barts for a week."

"I've been trapped in this house since 1991," Yvette Landish said. "That's over thirty years of suffering from a debilitating curse, Lucy. I would love to be in St. Barts. I would love to walk to the corner and back. Anything." There was real anguish in her mother's voice, and Lucy felt a rush of sympathy and concern as she thought of the long years that they'd *both* had to live with Yvette's agoraphobia.

"I know, Mom," she said gently. "I know." It was hard to tell yet whether Yvette was frustrated, confused, or just needed to vent.

"Why is this my life, Lucy?" A note of hysteria crept into Yvette's voice and the tears were evident. "I just want to be *normal*. And if I can't be normal, then what's the point of even being alive?"

Lucy ducked her head and closed her eyes. Her mother's level of need had been growing in recent years. Whereas once she had neighbors in Buffalo who indulged her requests for last minute items from the grocery store and who'd mowed her lawn for her and brought her mail to the door when they went out to retrieve their own, now she was surrounded by strangers with young children and unfamiliar last names. Her paranoia was also growing, and Lucy had received an alarming number of phone calls recently from her mother thinking that someone was trying to watch her through the windows (the UPS delivery man or a worker from the power company, usually). A recent diagnosis of dementia on top of everything else had further complicated Yvette's life, and, consequently, Lucy's.

"Mom," Lucy said, breathing in through her nose and out through her mouth. "I know this is hard and I'm sorry. I know I don't live close enough and—"

"*You left me, Lucy. You barely even *visit." There was a note of petulance and clear animosity in her mother's voice, and Lucy could hardly blame her. It was true: she'd jumped ship. Her husband had left her for a younger woman, she'd realized that her career was draining her, and the idea of becoming her mother's full-time caregiver and forsaking her own dreams had nearly crushed Lucy. So she'd hired people to help, enlisted her aunt Sharon's assistance, and then moved to Florida.

Lucy took yet another slow inhale and exhale before going on. "I visit as often as I can, and you knew that I'd be going on these trips all year long. We talked about this."

"Well, I don't think it's good for you to be so far away. What if something happens to me?"

Lucy massaged the spot on her forehead between her eyes; she could feel a headache pulsing there like a distant star.

"I have plenty of systems in place to make sure nothing happens to you."

"Oh, you're going to make your aunt Sharon babysit me?" Yvette spat. "No thank you."

"Aunt Sharon is your sister, Mom. She takes good care of you."

"I don't need my sister. I need my daughter."

Lucy gritted her teeth. "Mom, I'm doing my best. I promise you I am. I have to find the balance between looking after you and looking after me, and maybe I haven't gotten it right yet, but I am trying."

Yvette made a sound of disbelief. "In my time, children used to take care of their parents."

"Well, Mom," Lucy said, feeling resentment boiling up inside of her. "Times have changed and women aren't expected to give up on themselves and their dreams to raise children or to move in with their elderly parents. We go to college, we have careers, we can afford to hire other people to help us. I'm not perfect and I'm sorry if it's not the way you thought it would be, but I don't know how else to do this. I don't have all the answers." Without realizing it, her voice had gotten louder and the woman on the lounge chair nearest Lucy had put down her book to shoot a disapproving look her way. Lucy dropped her volume. "Listen, my life hasn't been perfect either. I'm a thirty-eight year old divorced woman trying to run a new business. I'm dealing with my own feelings of loneliness and dissatisfaction. I'm on this yearlong adventure not just for my business, but for myself. I'm trying my hardest to do right by both of us." She paused. "I love you, Mom," Lucy said more softly.

Yvette didn't respond and they both sat in silence for a moment.

"Now, I have people here on St. Barts to deal with, and I need to get back to it," Lucy said gently. "If you need me to do something, just let me know, okay?"

It was clear that Yvette was trying to think of some last little nugget of guilt to wedge under her daughter's skin, but instead she just sighed loudly. "Okay, I'll call you."

She hung up knowing that her mother would undoubtedly call— she'd call anytime the urge struck—and that her own feelings of helplessness in the face of her mother's condition would crop up and threaten to throw off her equilibrium if she let it. She just needed to hold steady for her own sanity.

Lucy slipped her phone into the pocket of her shorts, put a smile on her face, and turned back to where she and Finn had been sitting.

He was gone.

Their coffee cups sat on the table between the two lounge chairs, but no Finn. Her eyes skimmed the pool deck: women with books and oversized sunglasses; men in preppy sweaters; waiters in spotless white shorts and shirts. But no Finn.

COLOMBIER BEACH, AT THE NORTHERN TIP OF THE ISLAND, WAS ONE OF the most popular spots for snorkeling. Thirteen of the twenty-two Holiday Adventure Club travelers had signed up to join Lucy and Nick, and again they traveled by rented, chauffeured vans.

"This is the best place to see barracuda, green sea turtles, and stingray," the driver said in thickly accented English. The French influence was heavy in his voice and his eyes flicked at Lucy in the rearview mirror as he pulled into a makeshift parking spot near the beach. "If you stick to the northern side of the beach you will be protected from all the boats that come to moor here and you'll have a better time."

Lucy stood up halfway and tried not to bump her head against the roof of the van as she reached for the door handle. "Thank you so much. We'll probably be here for four hours, so I'm not sure if you want to wait or come back."

"I'll wait, *mademoiselle*," the driver said. He jumped out of the van and rushed around to her side, opening the sliding door and offering her his hand. Lucy took it and stepped down.

Within thirty minutes, all thirteen guests were standing on the sand, outfitted in rented snorkeling gear and listening to a brief overview from their guides, who had met them there. Samuel had a long, dark braid that fell down his bare back, and his wetsuit was unzipped to the waist and folded down, revealing an impressively well-formed set of abs and one arm that was completely tattooed from wrist to shoulder. His partner, Jana, was from Australia and couldn't have been more than four-foot-ten and 80 pounds. Lucy smiled as they played off of one another, giving instructions and making jokes with the group.

"I love that we're doing this," Nick said in a low voice, arms folded across his chest as he stood next to Lucy and listened to Samuel and Jana.

"Me too," Lucy whispered back. "It beats another day of

answering phones and shipping boxes while we drink coffee from Beans & Sand, huh?"

Nick was quiet for a minute and then he nodded slowly, keeping his eyes on the snorkeling instructors. "You miss Beans & Sand?" he asked, trying to sound casual.

Lucy knew he wasn't asking whether she missed the coffee shop that was on the other side of her travel agency, but if she missed its owner: dark, mysterious, sexy Dev Lopez.

Lucy took a beat to formulate her response. "I'm enjoying the coffee *here*," she finally whispered back, leaning closer to Nick's strong arm.

Things were always weird between her and Nick and Dev, and now that Nick had decided to tag along on this trip to St. Barts, it had thrown things off-balance with her and Dev. The same thing had happened when she'd attended the outdoor concert with Dev last month on Amelia Island, which had set up a few landmines for her and Nick to tiptoe around.

And yet despite all the romantic *potential* she had with both men, neither had actually made a concrete move. She hadn't kissed either of them, and while they clearly weren't the biggest fans of one another, it wasn't like they'd rolled up their sleeves and started duking it out over her affections.

And so Lucy stood next to Nick on a tropical island far from home and thought of Dev for a moment. But then she cut her eyes to Nick and admired his handsome profile. They were just so *different*. Nick, with his dreamy, rumpled, distracted professor appeal. The way he carried books with him everywhere and teased her good-naturedly. How he'd delicately averted his gaze the day before when the half-naked women passed by them at the pool. His charm and his manners were innate and tangible for Lucy, and there wasn't even a whiff of "bad boy" appeal about him. Nick was a one hundred percent, Grade A, what-you-see-is-what-you-get kind of guy.

But then there was Dev. Dark, dangerous, somewhat unknowable. He wasn't one for teasing, and his tough-to-please rock-and-roll persona presented the kind of challenge that many women would crawl on their knees for. Black leather pants, casually worn-in concert t-shirts, heavy boots. Lucy knew that he wasn't untamable (*Or was he?*), but he definitely gave off the vibe of a man who wouldn't roll over easily for anyone, and that alone was enough to intrigue a girl.

Nick glanced in her direction as the rest of the group followed Samual to the shoreline. "Yeah, the coffee here ain't half bad," he said, winking at her as Jana approached them.

"You two need to get suited up!" Jana called out, carrying two wetsuits for them.

Underwater, the world fell away and Lucy floated peacefully in the silence. The sea turtles scampered over coral reefs, and whenever she and Nick made eye contact, they waved excitedly. The flora and fauna bloomed before their eyes in bright reds, yellows, and oranges like pigment-rich oil paints squeezed from tubes. In the distance, a small airplane—a single-engine, two-seater Cessna—rested in the silt and sand at the bottom of the cove, its surfaces covered entirely by barnacles. They swam in that direction and went farther underwater in their full-face snorkel masks to check it out.

Even knowing that no one had died in the accident that sent this plane into the water, there was still something spooky and dark about peering through the dingy windows at the empty seats and algae-covered controls. A few fish swirled inside the plane's cabin and Lucy ran her hands over the bumpy surface of the aircraft; the barnacles made it feel as if she were reading Braille with her fingertips.

Nick reached for her hand and pulled her gently to the surface with him. They weren't suited up for full scuba diving, so it was impossible to stay under for too long.

"Wow," he said, pulling off his mask as soon as they broke the surface of the water. They treaded water side by side under the warm sun, looking around at the sparks of light that glittered on the turquoise waves. "This is amazing."

"Technically we could snorkel at home, you know," Lucy said. "But I guess that wouldn't be as exotic as snorkeling in the French West Indies, would it?"

"Definitely not." Nick adjusted his mask and let it rest on his forehead so that his face was in full view. He looked at Lucy for a long second and as he did, his hand brushed across her bare stomach beneath the water. She gave an involuntary shiver. "The weather might be similar, and the palm trees feel familiar, but ordering food off a menu where the prices are listed in Euros makes it feel like we're a million miles from home."

Lucy dipped her hair in the water and then let the excess water drip down the back of her neck. "Waking up to fresh papaya juice delivered to my door by a woman with a hibiscus behind one ear was my first clue that I'm in a different kind of paradise."

Nick laughed. "That's true. Normally Hemingway licks my face to wake me up after he's already licked himself, so a knock on the door from a woman bearing juice is a nice change."

Lucy laughed and looked toward the shore, where the rest of the snorkelers were conferring with Samuel and Jana. "Should we join them?" She'd momentarily forgotten that she and Nick weren't there alone, and while the tour group wasn't necessarily there to do everything together, she wanted to be careful not to appear as though she were trying to exclude them or leave them to fend for themselves.

As she stretched forward with both arms, ready to swim off in that direction, Nick reached for her waist and held her back lightly. "Hey, do you think maybe this evening we can have a drink on our own? After dinner or whatever? I don't want to take you away from the group or anything, but I'd love to have a little time with you."

The water was cold against Lucy's bare skin and Nick's fingers on her flesh felt hot and insistent. She looked into his eyes, trying to gauge his meaning but still just seeing Nick—her friend, her next door work neighbor, the cute guy she flirted with most week days—and so she smiled. "Yeah," she said, slipping from his grasp. "A drink. We can do that. It's a date."

With a wink, she swam to shore with Nick close behind.

5

MARCH 17
ST. BARTS

Finn had slipped away from the pool deck while Lucy was on the phone with her mother, her eyes fixed on the horizon far in the distance. He watched her for a minute, one hand on her hip, her foot kicking the base of the palm tree in a way that made her look like a teenager in trouble. He'd smiled at the image and then gotten ahold of himself; nurturing interest, however mild, in another woman was *not* why he'd come to St. Barts. In fact, that was entirely the opposite of the reason he'd taken the trip.

Within fifteen minutes, Finn had procured a small, boxy car painted mint green with white leather interior. Other than a glass windshield on the front, the car had plastic roll down shades that had been tied up to the roof, leaving the car wide open to the elements. The roof was a billowy canvas material, and Finn hopped in behind the wheel without even opening the low door, belting himself in quickly and pulling out of the hotel's lot and onto a long, winding road.

The air blew the fabric of his shirt in rippling waves and Finn rested his left wrist on the steering wheel as he drove, glancing out at the sparkling water and the blue sky. This is what he needed: open road and fresh air. Peace and quiet. No women.

A message from Carina floated through Finn's mind, as it had done at least a thousand times since she'd broken things off: *Finn... you've been the greatest gift a woman like me could ever hope to receive. But...*

Finn squinted his eyes, squeezed the steering wheel, and willed his brain to stop repeating *But...but...but.* Because really, there was no "but"—Carina had called things off between them. Carina with her wavy silver-blonde hair, her dancer's legs, the soft way her waist gave way to a real woman's body. It was true that they'd both had their reasons to keep things between them quiet, but Finn had never been afraid to take things to the next level. He'd never worried what people would think of them, and he'd looked forward to the day when he could proudly walk into any bar or restaurant with Carina on his arm and say to the hostess, "Two for dinner—it should be under Barlow."

But we come from two different places, Finn. Two different times. And those times and places don't necessarily overlap.

For Finn they had though. He'd always been considered an "old soul" and Carina was youthful and curious and she had that *laugh.* The kind of deep, knowing, full-body laugh that tickled his soul. And as for the places she'd spoken of? Who cared! Did it matter that she'd been born and raised in L.A. while Finn had grown up in the mountains? No. So what if she was a Valley Girl who grew up on punk rock, sunbathing with nothing on her skin but baby oil, and he'd been brought up in the forest with a fishing pole in hand and a Tamagotchi on his wrist. Carina had been raised during a time with no technology more advanced than a phone attached to her kitchen wall, and Finn had never known a life without a tiny computer in his pocket. Again—*who cared?* Not him. He'd never let their differences stress him out, and in fact, he'd been completely charmed by her lack of interest in some of the modern conveniences that he took for granted. Likewise, she'd let that gorgeous laugh loose on him more than once when he'd admitted that he'd never own a cassette tape and didn't understand the concept of a "collect call." So why had those things suddenly become liabilities? He didn't understand, and her letter didn't offer him any solid insight.

Finn shifted gears and pressed the gas pedal as he left town and wound around to the side of the island where there were fewer cars.

I've had things that you—if you stay with me—will never have, my love. I can't offer you life with a mate who will enjoy decades of perfect health. I cannot give you children. You will never know what it means to walk down the aisle toward someone who is also doing this thing called marriage for the first time. If you choose me, sweet boy, there are so many things I can't give you, and so many things that I'll take away from you.

Finn put both hands on the steering wheel and drove even faster. Give. Take. Love. Marriage. He didn't care and yet he cared so much that his eyes stung and burned. He wanted it all with *Carina* or he wanted none of it with *anyone.* It wasn't her right to decide for him what kind of storms he could weather, and it certainly wasn't within her capabilities to say that her health might fail or that in her absence he might find a woman who would enjoy a long and able-bodied life and give him a litter of perfect children. Just thinking of it now made him angry because neither one of them could know for certain *anything* that wasn't directly in front of their faces.

I never want to be a source of embarrassment for you; I don't want to be out in public, holding your hand and looking at you adoringly while people your age laugh at us. And I don't care if they laugh at ME, but it would break my heart to know that as I age I might make you look foolish. It would kill me, Finn—to be the source of any type of pain for you would absolutely break my heart.

But what about *this*? What about the pain it had caused him to find this note on his kitchen counter one evening after work instead of finding her purse and keys? To hear the empty silence of his house rather than her voice? Had she thought about how she was hurting him *now*?

Without any planning, Finn turned down a road that led toward the beach. He pulled into a sandy lot and shut off the car. Beyond the windshield, the morning sun played across the water and lit the scene with a yellow warmth. People walked up and down the sand, stopping and shielding their eyes as they watched yachts passing by. In the car, Finn gazed out, unseeing.

I can assure you that, at least in the short-term, this will be hard. Maybe impossible. But I know us and I know we can come out the other side and find ourselves again. For you that will mean falling in love and taking that other path...the one you're meant to take at your age. For me... who knows. But I won't ever find out if I stay. I love you, Finn Barlow. Whether this makes you question that fact or not, it still holds true: I love you and I always will.

The same feeling washed over Finn as he recalled the note nearly verbatim and went through it in his mind for what must be the thousandth time. He leaned his head against the headrest and closed his eyes, willing himself not to cry and not to give in to the rush of emotion that flooded him each time he remembered finding and reading the letter for the first time.

But in the end that wasn't entirely possible: the tears stayed in, but the feelings of loneliness and regret filled his chest to the point that he thought he might spontaneously combust. Life without Carina. Life without her voice reading books to him in bed late at night. Life without her love. None of it appealed to him at all, and despite his intention to come to St. Barts and move on, none of it was any less painful than it had been in California.

Finn turned over the engine of the little car and backed out of the lot.

6

MARCH 17
ST. BARTS

Lucy hadn't been sure at all that they'd find anything festive, but in the end, St. Barts had a few bars decked out for St. Paddy's Day, and along with a handful of the tour group members and Nick, she pushed through a heavy wooden door and found herself in the middle of what looked like a traditional Irish pub.

"Oh! I wasn't expecting this at all," she said, turning to Nick in surprise. The bar was long and made of polished wood, and along the mirrored back wall were several glowing sconces that made the bottles of liquor and the brass knobs of the draft beer tap shine in the low light. Tall bar chairs covered in tufted red velvet were taken up by patrons holding frosty mugs of beer and glasses of whiskey, and a band against the far wall was playing songs by the Irish band The Pogues.

Nick put both hands on Lucy's shoulders and gave her a little shake as he laughed. "You saw a sign out front that said 'Liam's Shamrock Pub' and didn't think that it might sort of lean in this direction?"

Lucy stuck her tongue out at him. They'd gone out for dinner as a smaller group than the night before, and Nick had reminded Lucy that they had a date for a drink that evening—just the two of them.

Several of their traveling companions had followed along cheerfully, but Lucy fully intended to come through on her promise and find a small table for two in a dark corner so that she and Nick could relax and not make small talk with strangers.

Sure enough, a scratched table with two empty chairs materialized when a group of burly men moved toward the bar. Lucy pointed at it wordlessly. Nick nodded at her and held up his fingers as if to ask if he should get two drinks. Rather than shout over the noise or make any requests, she gave him a thumbs-up and held her crossbody purse close against her stomach as she wove through the crowd and scored the table. She'd drink whatever he brought.

The band launched into a cover of The Pogues' "Eyes of an Angel" and Lucy turned her attention to them, nodding along as the lead singer leaned into the microphone and gave it his all.

"I got you a Guinness," Nick said loudly, holding up a pint of beer and setting it down on the table with a slosh. "It seemed fitting."

"That works." Lucy lifted the glass and knocked it against his, spilling even more onto the already wet and slightly sticky table before she took a sip.

It hit her then as they drank and listened to the band that they were sitting way too close to the music to actually carry on a conversation, and so they sipped their beers in amiable silence and watched the people around them. As soon as they'd both finished, Nick offered her a hand and pulled her to her feet.

"Are we leaving, or are we dancing?" Lucy said loudly, putting her mouth to his ear.

"Dancing first, then leaving," Nick said, tugging her to him without warning and causing her to give a little whoop. The men at the table next to theirs cheered as they watched the surprise on her face.

Nick started to do an exaggerated Irish jig as Lucy clapped her hands together, laughing. "You're not going to get away with just watching, lass," Nick said, wrapping one arm around her waist and taking her hand in the other.

Lucy had no choice but to hop along with him as the band played boisterously, until finally, out of breath and having laughed until her stomach hurt, Lucy grabbed Nick's hand and pulled him to the door.

Outside the sky was nearly dark and the street was full of people wandering and talking.

"You're quite the dancer." Lucy let go of his hand and fell into step beside Nick as they both caught their breath.

"Not really. I just know how to have a drink and cut loose. To be honest, I write better than I dance," he assured her. "At least, I hope I do."

"Oh, come on—don't sell yourself short. You're an amazing writer. But I wouldn't set my sights on *Dancing with the Stars* if I were you."

They walked past an ice cream shop that was completely full of people waiting for their cones, and then continued on down to the marina where some truly massive yachts bobbed in the water. Nick kept both hands in his pockets as they walked, which meant they successfully avoided that awkward hand-bumping thing that sometimes happened when you got too close to the person next to you.

"Let's sit," Nick said, lowering himself onto the wooden planks of the short pier and letting his legs hang over the side. The soles of his feet were just inches above the water and he offered Lucy a hand, helping her down as she sat next to him, legs dangling next to his own.

People moved around on the boats dotting the water in the marina and they watched them in silence, chuckling together as a man walked up onto the top deck of a huge yacht and grabbed his wife from behind, spinning her around enthusiastically as she shouted in happy surprise. On another boat, two young people—teenagers, they looked like from a distance—stood at the bow of a ship, watching the moonlight on the water before eventually coming together in a shy, halting kiss. They were so lost in one another that they were clearly unaware anyone might be able to observe them.

"So," Lucy said, nudging Nick with her elbow gently. "St. Patrick's Day on St. Barts. Was this anything you ever imagined yourself doing?"

"Nope," Nick admitted. "How about you?"

Lucy blew out a huge sigh. "Definitely not. My work life for the past decade mostly involved people who couldn't talk back to me, so dealing with real, live humans is a pretty big change. It's required a whole mental shift for me to think of myself as a travel agent and not a doctor."

Nick turned his head and looked at her. "Before you forget everything from med school, can you assess me? Do I have any classic disease symptoms I should know about?"

Lucy tucked her hands between her knees and laughed to herself. "No way," she said, shoulders shaking slightly as she considered the ridiculousness of her situation for about the eight millionth time. "I left that behind and broke that habit—I had to! I'm not Dr. Landish anymore, and I don't think I ever want to be again." She felt almost melancholy admitting this out loud; being a doctor had been her life's dream. Leaving her career had been a sad closure for her, but a necessary one. "I must have known deep down that the only way I'd ever escape the mess that my own life had become was to help people who want to escape theirs—even temporarily. Hence, the travel agency."

Nick stared at her for a long, quiet minute. "Is that how you see this?" He swept his hands around at the water and the sky. "As escaping your life?"

"Yeah. I guess I do." Lucy blinked a few times. "At least my old life. I think sometimes we outgrow the things that once fit us, and when we do, it's time to stretch. To change. To reinvent."

Nick nodded but said nothing, gazing out instead at the young couple who'd been kissing but were now just standing at the railing, the boy behind the girl, his arms wrapped around her waist as they looked out in peaceful contemplation.

Lucy felt her frustration over the phone call from her mother that morning building inside of her once again. "I mean, come on, Nick. I can barely live in a different city from my mom. She's on me *all the time* and I know that if I go back there it will kill me. I'll suffocate. As a reasonable adult who understands the concept of responsibility, I know I *should* be there, but I *can't*." Her throat tightened with every word, and she could almost feel the weight of her mother on her chest, crushing her ribs and stealing her breath. As the very thought of living in Buffalo and being sucked into her mother's daily needs washed over her, Lucy bent forward, putting her hands over her face and dropping her head toward her knees. "I'm trying to believe that in helping myself, I actually *am* helping her. And I hope I'm not wrong."

"Hey, hey," Nick said, sounding surprised. He placed one palm flat on her back and moved it in slow circles as she leaned forward. "Deep breaths. This was just a conversation, not a ringing indictment of you as a daughter. I see you every single day, Lucy. I see how hard you try, how much effort you put into everything you do. Even into helping your mom and being there for her."

Lucy sucked in air as she tried to slow her rapid, shallow breaths. "I know. It just starts to get to me sometimes." She brought her head up and let her hands fall so that Nick could see her blotchy face and the way she so easily went from a normal, functioning person to a completely unhinged child when the topic turned to the level of responsibility her mother required.

"That's okay," Nick reassured her, still rubbing her back gently. "We all have our stuff, and even though we've known each other for a while now, this isn't a topic we've really explored together. We worked through the Charlie and Katrina stuff—"

Lucy groaned out loud. "God, I can't believe I dumped all of that on you as well," she said, putting her hands to her cheeks again. "It wasn't even that big of a deal, I just didn't know many people on Amelia Island yet, and I—"

"Don't even worry about it. I was happy to listen, and I *am* always happy to listen to whatever you've got going on, Lucy."

Lucy turned to look at Nick full-on, her eyes searching his face. They were sitting closer than she'd realized and her heart picked up its pace again, though not from worrying about her mother this time. "Why are you so good to me?" she asked softly, looking into his warm eyes, at the way his cheekbones cut two sharp planes across his handsome face, and, finally, down at his soft lips. "Why do you put up with me and my nonsense?"

Nick stopped rubbing up near her shoulders and let his hand drift down to her lower back. The water beneath their feet lapped audibly against the wooden pier in a rhythmic pattern as they sat there, looking at one another intently. It was a moment where he could have said something major or said nothing at all and just let the feeling between them speak for him. It was a moment unlike any they'd shared before.

Lucy waited for him to say something or to kiss her or to pull her closer, and as she did, a sharp *splash* punctuated by a terrified shout filled the air and caused them both to jump. The moment vanished.

They looked at the water just in time to see the man who'd grabbed his wife in a playful embrace dive over the side of the yacht in one fluid, urgent motion and slice into the water.

Lucy sprang to her feet and Nick did the same. They stood and watched as the man surfaced once, then twice, and finally for a third time with his wife under one arm. Several people on their boat had come to the ledge and were waiting to throw them a flotation device, which the man hooked one arm through, allowing himself to be pulled toward the vessel as he held his wife under his other arm.

"Oh my god," Lucy said, shaking her head as people pulled the water-logged woman from the water and then offered the man a hand and pulled him back on board as well. "What the hell just happened?"

Nick looked on in amazement as people wrapped the man and the woman in huge towels and blankets. "Too much champagne, maybe?" He shrugged helplessly. "But it looks like it ended well."

"Thank god," Lucy said, already distracted by her own thoughts. Now that she knew things were fine with the couple, her mind instantly went back to the near-kiss she knew she'd almost shared with Nick. "They seem like they're in good hands." She moved her body so that she was facing him again, but instead of turning to her, Nick kept his body angled at the water and his eyes on the scene before them.

Lucy felt herself deflate. Even though they'd flirted and danced around one another for as long as they'd known each other, and even though they were now on this trip together, it seemed like they'd have to wait a bit longer before taking things any further. She took a step back from Nick and folded her arms across her chest as though she were suddenly cold.

"What do you think—should we head back to the bar and see if anyone is still there?" Lucy offered.

Nick finally turned to look at her and his face registered the realization that their moment had passed. "Oh," he said, running a hand through his hair. "Right. Yeah, let's head back."

Nick gave Lucy his arm and she took it, but it felt friendly again, not romantic. As they walked, they made small talk and it wasn't awkward or weird at all between them. Neither of them acknowledged the way they'd just nearly kissed on the pier, but Lucy couldn't help thinking of all the things that had led them to that moment: the way he'd given her a snow globe of Venice before her trip; the obvious jealousy between him and Dev when it came to Lucy; the fact that he'd even come on this trip at all.

This wasn't the time to search for clarity though, and Lucy knew that if and when it was ever time for them to figure things out, they'd figure them out. Until then, she'd just enjoy his company and friendship, and she'd try to hold her feelings about the situation with her mother at bay, where they belonged.

7

MARCH 18

ST. BARTS

Elise woke up to an onslaught of sunlight. It felt like the brightness might burn her retinas. She covered her face with both hands and rolled away from the open curtains. As she focused on the room around her, she felt a moment of confusion at the way things were configured. Both the dresser and door were in the wrong position. And the bathroom was on the opposite side of the room. She sat up, holding the sheet close to her body.

Wait—am I actually naked? She held out the sheet to confirm that she was, in fact, sleeping in the buff.

"Morning, sunshine," a male voice said from beyond the open doors to the balcony. "Sleep well?"

Elise's heart began to race and she clutched the sheet to her chest tightly. "Good morning," she ventured, hesitance written all over her face and in her voice. "I slept pretty hard."

The glow of sunlight was interrupted by the silhouetted figure of a tall man standing in the doorway. Elise squinted until the light adjusted and his face came into view: it was the man from the lobby on the first day of the trip. *Bradford*, she confirmed inside her head, trying to muster up a casual smile as she wracked her brain for some memory of the night before.

Bradford came and sat next to her on the bed. Miraculously, he looked showered, shaved, and ready to go and explore St. Barts in pressed linen shorts and a collared shirt. "I took the liberty of ordering us breakfast. It's on the balcony." He tipped his head at the white stone patio with its heavy railing and view of the water. Sunlight washed over the iron bistro table that was laden with china and sliver domed serving dishes.

"I need a shower." Elise sat up and put one hand over her mouth. "And I'm desperate to brush my teeth," she said, feeling suddenly shy and as if she'd just woken up naked next to a stranger. Which she had.

"Sure thing." Bradford stood up from the bed fluidly, giving Elise a chance to eyeball him. He was easily sixty, but had the posture and bearings of a man a decade or more younger. *Golf? Racquetball? Running?* she wondered, eyes grazing his muscular calves and broad shoulders as he walked into the bathroom.

He came back and thrust a fluffy, white terry cloth robe into her hands. "Here you go, milady. There's a new toothbrush and some toothpaste in the medicine cabinet." Bradford stood back and smiled widely, but made no move to look away so that Elise could modestly stand up and slip into the robe.

Wasn't he aware that women of a certain age didn't enjoy the way direct sunlight hit them, revealing every imperfection and wrinkle? She frowned at him, but as he continued to watch her with an open grin, she slid her arms into the robe awkwardly and then wrapped it around her body as she stood, mostly covering her skin as she trans-ferred herself to a standing position and knotted the robe around her midsection securely.

With the bathroom door locked firmly behind her, Elise flipped on the light and leaned closer to the mirror to examine her face. She was displeased to find a smear of mascara under each eye, hair that looked as though she'd run a marathon and then slept on the sweaty mess, and the kind of dry, wrinkled skin that comes from a night of too much alcohol and not enough water.

"Yuck," she said under her breath, opening the mirrored medicine cabinet. Sure enough, there was a toothbrush there in its packaging, which she unwrapped slowly, eyeballing the other items in the cabinet.

Bradford Melton was printed on several bottles of medication from a pharmacy in Chicago, though none of the prescription names were familiar to Elise aside from nitroglycerin, which seemed about right for a man his age. She closed the cabinet and was faced with her own reflection once again.

Had she really done this? Met a man, decided he might have what she needed, and gone directly up to his hotel room with him? As she glanced around, noticing the black comb he'd left on the wash basin and the damp towel hooked on the back of the bathroom door, Elise imagined briefly that Bradford was actually her husband or her boyfriend, and that this is what it would be like to travel with a man again. She'd wake up each morning to room service and a robe handed to her by someone gorgeous and wealthy, and the rest of the things that weighed her down in life would fade, becoming minor details she could manage rather than seemingly insurmountable stressors.

After washing her face with a washcloth and running Bradford's comb through her hair, Elise tied the robe tighter and straightened her shoulders. She honestly couldn't quite remember how wild things had gotten the night before, but she clearly had nothing to be ashamed of. It wasn't as if he'd sent her away after their tryst, and it was clear that even now he wanted her to stay and have breakfast and coffee.

As she walked out onto the balcony, Bradford folded and lowered the newspaper he was looking at, resting it on the knee that he'd crossed over his other leg.

"Let me pour you some coffee," he said with a knowing smile, looking her over as he reached for a mug and saucer and the carafe of coffee. "Sugar or cream?"

"Both, please," Elise said, feeling shy. She sank into a cushioned chair across from him and adjusted her eyes to the morning light yet again. "This is gorgeous," she added, sweeping a manicured hand across the horizon. The water was turquoise and inviting, and beyond the beach that fronted the hotel, a handful of yachts with colorful sails bobbed gently on the water like confetti sprinkled from above.

Bradford looked out at the water. "It's not too shabby," he agreed, though he didn't sound nearly as impressed as Elise felt. "I come here every year, but I will say that this year is off to a much more exciting start than years past." One of his eyebrows lifted playfully.

Elise accepted the coffee gratefully and took her first sip. "I like you, Bradford," she said, wishing instantly that she'd said something less forward to him as she sat there in a robe with no makeup and no idea about whether she'd done anything to embarrass herself the night before.

To his credit, Bradford laughed, but in a way that told her he was charmed and not simply amused by her girlish outburst. "You're pretty okay yourself, kid," he said, winking at her and picking up his newspaper again. "Hey," he said, peeking at her over the edge of the sports page. "I'm having a little reception on my boat tonight, and I'm hoping you'll be my date."

Elise paused, coffee cup held between both hands and poised at the edge of her lips. She looked at him long and hard. "You mean...on your yacht?"

Bradford chuckled, but looked slightly confused. "Yes, on my yacht. I told you last night at dinner that I was here for the regatta, and tonight is the official owner's reception, where people can basically party hop between one another's boats." His eyes twinkled as he watched her face. "So, will you come?"

Elise clutched at the fabric of her robe, holding it closed across the deep V of her cleavage. "Yes," she said, feeling excitement bubbling up inside of her. "I will definitely come."

"So listen, honey." Elise was following Finn across the lobby in her kitten heels. "I really think you should come tonight."

Finn's eyebrows shot up as he reached the front counter and

glanced over at Elise. He rested his elbows on the marble counter, waiting for the concierge to finish with a phone call.

"You want me to go on your date with you tonight?"

Elise laughed and waved a hand. Her gold bangle bracelets jangled. "No, no, no! I'm inviting you along to the owner's reception on Bradford's yacht." She searched his face, hoping that he might realize the importance of the fact that she'd been on the island for less than 48 hours and had already secured a date with an *extremely* impressive man. Instead, he just looked confused.

"I mean...yeah," Finn said, clasping his hands together and leaning his weight on his forearms. He stared at the concierge's back as if this might force him to wrap up the phone call and give Finn his full attention. "I could come along. I don't really have any other plans for the evening."

The giant fans overhead were made of bamboo shaped into palm fronds, and they turned slowly, creating a slight breeze that ruffled the potted plants scattered around the lobby.

"Okay, wonderful!" Elise grabbed his arm excitedly. "You're in room 513, right?"

Finn nodded, glancing at her quickly before turning his attention back to the concierge.

"Then I'll come by later and slide an invitation under your door." She watched him, mystified by how distracted he seemed.

"Okay." Finn nodded.

Without waiting for more, Elise walked away.

"Sir, thank you for your patience," the concierge on duty said, setting the phone back in its cradle and giving Finn a half-smile. He wore a starched white shirt with a name tag that said Etienne. "How may I assist you?"

Finn rocked back on his heels and lifted his hands from the counter. "Yes. Hi. I was wondering if there was any sort of paragliding or zip-lining or anything I could sign up for this afternoon."

"Yes, sir," Etienne said, pulling a binder full of pamphlets from under the counter. "I'm happy to give you some ideas of activities you can do here on St. Barts."

When Finn left the front desk a few minutes later, he had a handful of brochures for a variety of bike tours, historical sites, and private beaches. A jazzy French song played in the lobby and Finn stopped at the edge of the open area, looking out at the pool. He slid his aviator sunglasses on and watched as wealthy older couples looked at one another with the kind of calm confidence that comes from not having a single material concern in the world. He imagined that they were discussing what kind of champagne went best with sea scallops, or where they'd take their ski vacation next winter. In his hand he had information for several things he could do with his time, but in his heart he had no desire to do any of them.

Finn glanced down at the brochure on the top of the pile: a trip to the Wall House, an historic site that highlighted the island's Swedish colonial era. He shuffled to the next one: Shell Beach. Next: paddle boarding or kiteboarding with a local company. Finn shoved the brochures into the back pocket of his cargo shorts with a sigh. It had seemed like a good idea to get out and do something active, but instead all he wanted to do was call Carina. To send her a picture of the water and tell her he wished she was here.

What was that thing he'd heard about from one of the guys he worked with whose daughter was struggling with an eating disorder? Some sort of therapy that dealt with cognitive behavior changes? As in, *let's replace your negative or pervasive thoughts with something else.* If the guy's daughter could replace thoughts of starving herself with something that made her happy, couldn't he do the same thing with Carina? He closed his eyes behind his shades and tried to push the image of her from his mind, replacing it instead with one of him on his own, sitting in a kayak with a smile on his face and the wind in his hair.

It lasted for a whole half-second before vanishing and morphing into a scene of Carina running her fingers through his hair as he lay next to her on a Sunday morning. Then another of them having lunch at a cafe near the beach in Carmel once when they'd taken a long weekend together. With a shake of his head, Finn opened his eyes and turned away from the pool in frustration. He strode through the lobby, stopping in front of a highly-polished brass trash can to pull the pamphlets from his back pocket and slip them through the garbage can's flap. This vacation was nothing more than a painful diversion from dealing with the reality of his situation, and so far it had been largely unsuccessful. He'd quickly come to realize that there was no such thing as running away, because no matter where he went, Carina went with him.

Tonight he'd go to the owner's reception with Elise, and tomorrow he'd catch a flight home.

MARCH 18

ST. BARTS

A row of yachts that surely had the collective value of a small third-world country lined the marina, looking to all who passed by like floating piles of money and class.

Lucy had run into Elise earlier in the day and because Nick had started to feel under the weather that afternoon, Lucy had been easily convinced to drop by the owner's reception by herself after dinner. Now, wearing a cream-colored wrap dress and matching strappy sandals, she held her purple sequined clutch under one arm and the invitation to the event printed on hard card stock in the other hand. Overhead, lamps that lit the wooden pier glowed against the darkening sky.

"I hope you're coming aboard!" A man her age wearing a loose linen blazer with a mostly unbuttoned silk shirt beneath it called out from a deck that looked down to where Lucy stood. "Yes," he called out, cupping his mouth with both hands and nodding at her, "I'm talking to you, gorgeous!"

Lucy felt her face flame and she smiled up at him, feeling mostly entertained by his drunken attention. Normally she would be more annoyed by an inebriated stranger shouting at her, but there was something about this evening that made her feel like she wasn't quite herself. Instead, she was a looser, more carefree version of Lucy Landish, open to possibility and willing to see where the path led her.

With a laugh, Lucy looked right back at him. "But you don't even know me," she called back, switching her purple clutch so that it was wedged under the other arm.

"Yet," the man corrected her. "I don't know you *yet*."

Lucy considered walking past the boat, as the yacht she was looking for—the one Elise's new boyfriend/vacation-fling was throwing the party on—was called *Mischief at Sea* and this one was emblazoned with the cheeky moniker *Mortimer's Melons*. Her eyes grazed the side of the boat as the man watched her.

"No," he called down, waving both hands at her as he shook his head, "ignore the name of this vessel. It belongs to my Uncle Mort and he's a randy old perv. Wait right there, okay? Just wait!"

As Lucy stood there debating whether or not to walk on, the man disappeared into the center of the boat, descended via some unseen stairs, and emerged on the bottom deck, where he used a step ladder to turn and lower himself onto the pier.

"Hi," he said, walking toward her with a hand extended. "Philippe. But you can call me Eep."

"Eep?" Lucy shook his hand. The nickname actually made her laugh out loud.

"Yeah, short for Philippe. You know." He shrugged, letting go of her hand as he tossed his loose hair easily out of his eye with a shake of his head. "Boarding school nickname. It stuck."

"I see," Lucy said. "Well, I'm Lucy. It's the name my mom gave me. It stuck."

Eep chuckled. "You're a keeper. Can I invite you aboard *Mortimer's Melons* for a glass of champagne?"

Lucy looked up and down the pier, watching as people made merry and wandered on and off the docked yachts. "Well," she said, hesitating for a second, "I'm supposed to be meeting a friend on a boat called *Mischief at Sea*—"

"Ah, Bradford Melton," he said, nodding. "A friend of my father's."

Lucy frowned, disbelieving. "Do all of you know one another?"

"You mean all the children of rich old dudes? Or everyone who owns a yacht?" Eep held out a hand and led Lucy to the step ladder, which she looked at dubiously. "Here, I'll help you up," he said.

"I just meant everyone who comes to St. Barts for the regatta," she clarified, handing him her clutch purse and using both hands to hoist herself up onto the three-step ladder, which she stood on gingerly in her heels as the wind blew the back of her dress up slightly. "Oh!" Lucy said, using one hand to hold down her dress.

"Here," Eep said, turning his back to her. "I promise I won't look as you climb on, and as soon as you're aboard, I'll follow you up."

"You're not going to run off with my purse?" Lucy teased, stepping over the low lip of the boat and finding herself on solid ground again.

"I wouldn't dream of it," Eep promised as he climbed up the ladder.

On the boat, people mingled and talked in low voices. Eep held up a finger and a waiter in white pants and a white shirt approached with a tray in hand. "Sir?" he asked.

"Two glasses of champagne, please," Eep said, nodding a wordless hello to a man who was standing about thirty feet away in a navy blazer and shorts that showed off deeply tanned legs. "Have you eaten?" he asked Lucy, looking at her appraisingly. "In my experience, a woman of your alluring yet slight physique can't hold much champagne without a little bread or something to soak it up. Shall I get us some cheese and crackers?"

He was purposely using an exaggerated tone and words to sound debonair, and the overall effect was fairly amusing. It felt like old-fashioned charm to Lucy, and as she looked around, imagining Eep at boarding school, it was easy to picture him learning about etiquette and manners from another time.

"I ate," Lucy said, taking the champagne as the waiter came back and offered them two glasses on his tray. "Thank you."

"So tell me about you, Lucy. Where are you from?"

"Florida," she said, sipping the champagne. "You?"

"Boston. I've been to Florida though. Palm Beach. Miami. Tampa."

"Of course," she said, giving him a noncommittal smile. It was rare to meet anyone on planet Earth who hadn't been to Miami. "I've never been to Boston."

"Harvard. Snows a lot. Aerosmith. Lots of *pahking* the *cah* in the *yahd*," he added with a wink, quickly switching from his crisp, flat boarding school accent to a more regional one.

"Ah, I'm sure your parents spent good money with dialect coaches to pave over that accent," she joked. There was no doubt in her mind that no matter how many generations Philippe's family went back in Boston, not a single person ever said *cah* or *yahd*.

"Indeed," Eep said, tipping back his champagne and draining the glass. "Now, let's talk more about you." He set his empty glass on the tray of the same waiter as he passed by and then took Lucy's elbow, leading her smoothly to a set of stairs that led to a higher deck. "Do you like looking at the stars?"

Lucy laughed. "Smooth," she said, letting herself be led. "Like *buttah.*"

It was Eep's turn to laugh as he placed a hand on her lower back and walked her up towards the stars and the night sky above.

"Isn't this *magical*?" Elise said, both hands on Finn's left arm as she stood next to him on the *Mishief at Sea.* "I had no idea that Bradford owned a yacht like *this.*" She dropped her voice and leaned closer to Finn. "But in addition to the money, he's also really nice." Her eyes searched Finn's face. "Do you think this is too fast? To fall for someone?"

Finn blinked a few times as he looked down at the woman he'd met on an airplane just a couple of days before. She was easily old enough to be his mother, if not his grandmother, and giving her relationship advice felt weird. "I'm not sure," he said honestly, wishing— and not for the first time since making his way to the marina—that he'd taken a flight home that very afternoon rather than waiting for the next day. "I mean, are you really just looking for a rich guy, or is there something more you want?"

Elise, still holding onto his arm, yanked it and gave him a loud "*Hush!*" as she pulled him further away from any of the other guests. "I'm not *just* into him for the money," she said, looking around as she spoke. "But I *do* need a man with some money, Finn. That's just the realistic fact of my situation. And Bradford...well, he seems really wonderful."

Finn nodded, listening but also thinking of Carina and the realistic facts of his own situation. Was it even possible not to do that? To listen to someone without thinking about your own stuff as your mind wandered? He forced himself to focus on her face.

"I'm glad. I guess I would say that you should be careful. I mean, we don't really get to know another person overnight, and it's possible he's just looking to have a good time while he's here."

Elise chewed on her lower lip as she listened. "You're right. You're so right," she said, clearly weighing his male insight into the situation. "I'll watch myself. But now," Elise patted his arm firmly, "what about you? You got your eye on any ladies yet?"

Finn shook his head vehemently. "Nope. Just like I told you on the plane, I'm here to get over a lady. I don't want to find a new one. And I'm actually thinking of leaving tomorrow—this just isn't working out for me."

"Mmmm." Elise squinted at him. "I see." She fluffed her red hair as she watched his face. "Well, let's get you a drink, shall we? See if we can't change your mind and make you stay?"

"You're a very persuasive woman, Elise," Finn said, following her to the bar at one end of the yacht. "But I don't think you'll convince me to stay."

Elise grinned at him slyly. "We'll see, Captain," she said, handing him a cocktail. "We'll see."

☙

Lucy had extracted herself from Eep with a promise to call him at the number he'd insisted on putting into her phone, but she had no intention of actually doing so. Being invited onto a yacht by a stranger had been a fun departure from real life and real responsibilities, but Lucy knew it was time to get back to the task at hand.

After three flutes of champagne and two bites of caviar on toast, Lucy had tired of the women wearing jewelry that cost more than her first car (or, in some cases, more than her current car combined with her Amelia Island bungalow), and she grew bored of watching the older men preen for the younger women, gently and absentmindedly touching their hair plugs to make sure the wind hadn't blown their carefully cultivated strands askew.

It was all a great big show, Lucy had realized as the alcohol warmed her: the older men grasped at their own lost youth and clamored for the attention of the young, nubile females in attendance. The women of all ages, for their part, were hungrily eyeballing the firm, chiseled servers as they rotated across the yacht's polished deck, offering drinks and sexy smiles, but when it came time to engage in conversation and flirtation, the women shored up their reserves and turned to the moneyed older gentlemen, ignoring the slight hunch to the men's aging shoulders and focusing instead on what they presumed were their extremely robust bank accounts.

Nothing about it appealed to Lucy. Eep—though relatively close to her age—had the devil-may-care rakishness of a playboy on the make, and while Lucy had been marginally flattered by his attention, there was nothing as appealing about him as the things that drew her to say, Nick. Or Dev. She wandered down the pier now, not so much weaving as walking more slowly and with a looser gait after the champagne, and as she did, she thought about Nick. She'd left him in his room with the promise to call or text her immediately if he started to feel worse, and as she remembered this, she stopped to fish her phone from her clutch purse and check her messages.

Nothing from Nick, she saw as she scrolled through her texts. There was one short missive from Carmen in the group chat with her and Bree (they'd been carrying on a conversation since returning from Venice, and her fun new friendship with two women she'd only known for just over a month was something she already cherished), and, shockingly, a photo from Dev.

She clicked on the message from Dev to open it fully.

Bonjour, the text said. *(That's because you're in the French West Indies.) I don't want you to worry, but there was a burglary in the strip mall last night and they hit Honey's nail salon. Broke her window and stole some of her equipment and cash. The rest of us are unscathed. I'll keep you posted if anything else comes of it.*

Lucy sucked in a sharp breath as she opened the photo he'd attached: it was a shot of Honey's salon, the front window smashed and glass scattered all over the linoleum floor inside. The pedicure chairs and manicure stations were empty, but it looked as if someone had taken a hand and swept the hundreds of bottles of nail polish off the shelves on the wall, scattering them everywhere.

"Oh, no..." Lucy put a hand to her mouth as she surveyed the mess. She felt horrible for Honey, a single older woman running her own business. Truth be told, she saw her own future when she looked at Honey. Not that she fancied herself a psychic, as Honey did, or that she'd end up giving manicures and pedicures in her own sunset years, but as a woman who ran a business and lived alone, it sometimes felt as if the world was out to get you. Or at least as if it wasn't there to support you when you needed it. And this break-in was further proof to Lucy that you had to stay strong and stay aware. Never turn your back on the ocean. Don't trust anyone.

She wavered just slightly on her heels and closed the message, dropping her phone back into her purse. *Okay, I might have had one glass too many*, she thought to herself, looking up and down the marina. She started walking again, and with just a few quick inquiries of the people passing her by, Lucy had been directed to the *Mischief at Sea*, which stood tall and proud and blazing with light against a navy blue sky. From the speakers on deck she could hear the strains of Christopher Cross singing "Arthur's Theme" (*Classic yacht rock*, she thought) and the tinkle of female laughter as yet another group of women vied for the attention of the wealthy men aboard the boat.

Once on board, Lucy accepted a multi-hued frozen cocktail from a young woman in a tight red halter top and black shorts. She was wearing a jauntily tipped sailor's cap and her curly hair was gathered in a low ponytail.

"Thanks," Lucy said, using the straw in the drink to blend the crushed ice and the liquor. She took a sip and looked around.

"Hey," a voice said as a hand touched her elbow. "A familiar face."

"Oh!" Lucy spun around and found herself looking directly into Finn Barlow's clear eyes. "Finn—hi." Finn was holding the same drink in his hand that Lucy was holding in hers, and without thinking, she tipped her glass in his direction. "Cheers," she said. "To Elise's wild love life and the fact that we get to hang out on a multi-million dollar yacht tonight because of her."

Finn clinked his glass against hers. "Yeah, to Elise." He sipped his drink, but he looked decidedly mellow as he glanced around. "Hey," he said, turning his attention back to Lucy. "By the way, sorry I bolted on you at the pool yesterday. I wasn't trying to be rude."

Lucy felt herself pull back in surprise. "God, Finn," she said, shaking her head. "Please—you don't need to apologize. You're here for a good time and that's all I'm concerned about."

"Well," he said, but he stopped there.

Lucy could feel the awkwardness in his pause. "Anyway," she pushed on, stirring her drink again with the straw to avoid taking a big, frozen sip and rendering her brain a useless glacier in her skull. "How have things been going so far?"

Finn's jaw clenched and he breathed in through his nostrils. "Not great," he admitted. "I came here to get over someone and it's not going exactly as planned."

"Ahhh." Lucy pressed her lips together as she nodded. She knew about trying to get over someone, and she also knew that there was no magic bullet to make it happen. "You're bringing it up, but I don't know you well enough to know whether you just wanted to say it, or whether you actually want to talk about it, so I'm going to follow your lead."

Without discussing it, they started to amble towards the empty bow of the yacht, leaning forward with their elbows onto the railing and holding their drinks but not sipping them.

"I guess I want to talk about it," Finn acquiesced. "Or talk about her. Us. I don't know."

Lucy waited patiently, looking out at the water to give him some space.

"Her name is Carina. She's fifty-one." He went quiet, letting that settle and perhaps anticipating a response from Lucy, but she gave none. "I'll be thirty this summer, so obviously there are a few years between us," he said wryly. "I'm in love with her and she broke things off because she thinks there are too many obstacles for us to overcome."

"Mmm," Lucy said, nodding slightly but still not looking at him. "I see."

"I wanted to go out on the town together. To let everyone see what we had because it's amazing and she's my everything." His voice sounded anguished as he pushed off of the railing and stood upright, still holding the frozen drink. "I have nothing to be ashamed of. I don't care if we grew up in different times, and I don't care if people think twenty years is too much. We're adults."

Lucy inhaled deeply. "But?"

Finn examined the drink in his hand as if he'd just remembered it was there. "But she was my high school English teacher."

"Eek." This response was unavoidable, but Lucy let it slip like a tiny squeak, not a horrified shriek. Finn was, after all, a thirty-year-old man. He could date whomever he wanted.

"Yeah, but that's not a big deal, Lucy," Finn said, turning to face her. "I can guarantee you that *nothing* happened back then. She wasn't even my favorite teacher, just a really nice lady. I graduated, went to college, became a firefighter, and then about a year ago we ended up at the same retirement party in a bar and recognized each other. We caught up, then one thing led to another. I don't even see how there's a problem with a man who's nearly thirty dating a woman who just happened to be his teacher over a decade ago."

"But she does?" Lucy ventured.

Finn shrugged. "She says there's a 'whiff of impropriety' to it and that kind of freaks her out when it comes to other people knowing. But when it's just the two of us, it's obviously not a problem."

"Okay, that's fair. She's just worried about how things might look, although to an outsider, I can agree with you that it sounds as if there's absolutely nothing to be worried about as far as either facts or perception."

Finn took a long pull of his drink. "Yeah, well, Whitefish is a small town. People talk. And she says she's mostly worried about me. About the things I'm giving up: children, a long life with a woman my own age—things I'm not even asking her for!"

"I think those are fair things to worry about," Lucy said, standing upright and facing him now that he'd started talking freely. "As a woman, I can tell you that the ability to give a man children, should the opportunity and desire arise, are pretty important. They go soul-deep, you know? It hits you here," she said, balling her hand into a fist and tapping it against her heart as her eyes filled with involuntary tears. "Taking away future happiness from someone you truly love is not something to be taken lightly."

"But *she* is my future happiness. Not some kids I don't even know or want yet. And all those little details that people seem to think would make or break a relationship with an age gap like ours? They're *nothing*," he said emphatically. "Just because she can remember where she was on 9/11 and I can't doesn't define us or determine whether or not we're compatible. When I make jokes about things that aren't on her radar, it's no big deal. We explain things to each other all the time and we both think it enhances who we are as people. So I just don't see how there's a problem."

"Yeah," Lucy said, giving him a "beats me" face and a shrug. "I'm with you on this, Finn. It sounds like yes, there's a semi-dramatic age gap here that could cause some heartache, but ultimately you sound like two people who really enjoy each other's company and you have no reason to hide that."

Finn stared at her, relief etched all over his handsome face. "Thank you for saying that. Other than briefly mentioning my break-up to Elise on the airplane, you're the first person I've really laid this out for. I can't tell anyone back home because Carina and I agreed not to, so I've been living in this sort of...vacuum. Just wondering whether I'm crazy to feel so strongly about the rightness of this when she clearly thinks there are hurdles we can't clear. Sometimes I feel like I'm losing my mind."

Lucy put a hand on Finn's strong forearm. "I don't think you're crazy, Finn. I think you sound like a man in love."

Finn looked out at the dark water and then up at the moon. "Can I buy you a drink, Lucy? For being such a good listener?"

She laughed. "I think they're free."

"Then let me procure you a free drink," Finn said, leading her back toward the waitresses with the frozen cocktails. "Because we're at an owner's reception on St. Barts during the regatta, and there's no reason for us not to have all the free drinks we want."

"You know," Lucy said, walking next to him amiably, "you are so, so right, Finn."

THE PARTY WAS IN FULL SWING AND ELISE WAS HOLDING COURT WITH Bradford Melton as he told what seemed to be hilarious stories to a small crowd when Lucy was accosted by a very small woman with a thick German accent.

"*You!*" the woman shouted, pointing at Lucy. "I need to see you in my gown."

"Pardon me?" Lucy turned to Finn automatically to see if maybe he'd understood something that she hadn't. Finn gave her a blank look. Unfortunately, they'd both carried on with the frozen cocktails and neither of them seemed to be very clear on anything at that exact moment.

"I have a gown that would be perfect for you. Just perfect." She reached out and took Lucy by the wrist with a grasp much firmer than seemed possible for a woman her size. Lucy realized immediately that this tiny woman was *that* girl on the playground—everyone knew the girl—who was small but tough and a little mean. The one who grabbed you hard and pinched you when no one was looking to make sure you knew that she was always going to get her way.

"Um, okay. A gown." In her slightly inebriated state, Lucy let herself be dragged to a set of stairs that led down to the lower deck of the yacht.

As they walked down a narrow, dimly-lit hallway, Lucy reached out a hand to touch the woman's arm. "Wait. Who are you?" she asked, frowning. She turned to look behind her to see whether Finn had followed them; he had not.

"Astrid," the woman said crisply, stopping in front of a door. "I am a friend of Bradford's."

"Oh. I'm Lucy," Lucy said, swaying slightly, though she was unsure whether it was her who was swaying or the boat. Maybe both.

"You are gorgeous." Astrid threw open the door to a stateroom and stood to one side so that Lucy could enter. "You have fabulous hair and that tanned skin will look amazing with my gown."

"I live in Florida," Lucy said by way of explanation, stifling a burp as she felt the alcohol slosh around in her stomach. She took in the details of Astrid's room: queen-sized bed with expensive looking white bedding; lamps with navy blue shades on each side of the bed, both switched on and casting a warm glow; a framed painting of a regatta on the wall; an oversized porthole window that looked out into the dark night.

"Here," Astrid said, opening a narrow closet and pulling out two zippered garment bags. She set them both on the bed, side by side, and opened them one at a time. From the first bag she pulled a cream-colored tulle dress that looked like the frosting on top of a cupcake. Lucy made an awed sound.

"What are these for?" she asked, setting her sequined purse on the foot of the bed and leaning closer to admire the dress.

"They are for my fall/winter line, Lucy," Astrid said, unzipping the second dress and revealing a satin sheath in the palest shade of blue that Lucy had ever seen.

"What line?"

Astrid sighed, but not impatiently. "Have you heard of Astrid Lindt Bridal?"

Lucy shook her head, feeling dumb. Weddings had never really been her thing, even when she'd been planning her own, but she *had* heard of Vera Wang, if not simply because of her fame in the bridal world, then because of the years she'd been famous for her creations. Beyond that though, she was lost on all things bridal. In fact, her ex-husband's mother and sister had planned most of her wedding, and she'd been completely fine with it.

"I make wedding dresses. Many different wedding dresses. And these are my two favorites," Astrid said distractedly, looking at the two gowns with pride as if she were a mother watching her young perform some amazing feat.

"They're beautiful," Lucy whispered with reverence.

"Would you try this one on for me? Please?" Astrid looked at her with unbridled hopefulness. "I wanted to show them off while I was here on St. Barts, but the model I'd invited decided not to come at the last minute. We had a photo shoot planned and everything."

"I'm sorry." Lucy looked at Astrid as she ran the tips of her fingers over the pale blue satin. Astrid looked to be about fifty, but she had the small, muscled body of a teenage gymnast. "I hope her agency like, punishes her. Or whatever. I'm not really sure how the whole model thing works," she added, feeling inadequate in the face of all this fashion and glamour.

"Well." Astrid's eyes flickered with a spark. "We had a...personal relationship. And apparently that has ended. So." She lifted her eyebrows, but it was clear that she didn't feel all that nonchalant about the situation.

"Oh," Lucy said, understanding her meaning. "Then I'm sorry for that too. But I'm not sure these dresses will fit me—"

"They will." Astrid was firm. "Here." She lifted the cream tulle dress and thrust it at Lucy. "This one, please."

Lucy reached up with one hand and scratched the back of her neck, trying to buy time. "I don't know, Astrid. I was actually going to leave the party soon. My friend Nick came with me from Florida, and he got sick this evening, so I—"

Astrid cut her off with a wave of the hand. "I will not hear no for an answer."

Lucy took a deep breath. "Okay. I guess I could just try it on really fast." She could have easily forced herself out of the room and back up the stairs, but even Lucy could admit that there was something flattering about a designer begging to see her in one of the upcoming season's creations.

"Those shoes you have on are perfect." Astrid nodded at the cream-colored strappy sandal-heels that Lucy was wearing. "Let's just get you out of that dress."

Before she could give it more thought, Lucy found herself standing in the middle of Astrid's room in nothing but a lacy bra and a pair of satin panties. Thank god they matched her dress; she'd had no intention of disrobing in front of anyone, but it never hurt to wear the kind of underwear you wouldn't mind having EMTs see you in after a horrible accident. Even in her slightly altered state she could call on the dark humor and sober wisdom she'd gleaned during her years as a doctor.

"Here. Turn." Astrid had her step into the dress, which she'd set in a pile on the floor, opening the bodice so that there was a distinct hole for Lucy to step into. She pulled the tulle carefully up the length of Lucy's body, offering her the two straps to put her arms through, and now she stood behind her, ready to zip the gown and reveal to Lucy what she'd look like as a slightly drunken, surprised bride.

"My god," Lucy said, turning and catching her own image in the full-length mirror on the back of the bathroom door. She looked like Carrie Bradshaw in Paris on *Sex & the City*. She looked like a cloud. A meringue. Like whipped cream and angel hair and a Victoria's Secret model in the kind of dress that she imagined one of them might wear to the altar. "It's...wow."

Astrid's smile was small and tight, and her face stayed focused as she looked at Lucy, taking in the full picture. "Hair down," she said, reaching up without permission and pulling the pins from Lucy's haphazard bun. Her auburn hair spilled over her shoulders, and all at once she became a bride. "Yes. Like that."

Astrid stood back and looked at her for a moment. "Let's go upstairs."

"Oh," Lucy said, holding out her hands. "No. No, I don't think so."

"Yes, Lucy. We will go." Astrid opened the door and marched out, not waiting for Lucy to make up her mind.

Grabbing the voluminous tulle gown in both hands, Lucy muttered about what she'd gotten herself into, but she followed Astrid anyway.

Upstairs, the guests stopped talking and turned to ooh and ahh at Lucy, who emerged to a smattering of unexpected applause.

"My best creation for the next wedding season," Astrid said loudly, cupping her hands around her mouth as someone turned down the music. "My friend Lucy is here to model it for us."

Lucy blushed furiously, feeling all eyes on her. She dropped the tulle fabric and it settled around her. For a moment, she felt like a Barbie doll, but the discomfort of being watched persisted and she realized that this was exactly why she'd never done anything where she would be the center of attention. No high school dance team, no acting in school plays, no performing whatsoever. The solitude of her former career washed over her as she realized that, professionally, anyway, she'd gone from standing with a scalpel in one hand and a body before her, to drinking champagne on yachts and modeling wedding gowns.

"Come and walk for us, darling," a much older woman said, waving her gnarled hands to indicate that Lucy should move and show off the gown. The woman's nails were polished a shiny coral color, and on several fingers she wore rings with diamonds so large that they swayed along with the movement of her hands.

There was a brief hesitation—a moment where Lucy considered turning around and going back the way she'd come, fleeing back to Astrid's stateroom where she could shed this dress and change back into her own. She'd sobered up enough in the past twenty minutes to realize that this was not something she would normally be doing, and besides, she really needed to check on Nick. She needed to show him the picture Dev had sent and tell him about the break-in back home and that everything was fine.

But just as she was about to turn and descend the stairs, Finn appeared, arm held out gallantly. "Allow me to escort you," he said, smiling and looking fairly entertained. "I had no idea I'd been drinking with a supermodel all evening."

"Ugh," Lucy said, taking his arm. "As if." There was no going back now. They crossed the deck with the tulle train dragging behind her. It all seemed so bizarre as she glanced around, taking in the appreciative looks of the guests on the yacht. *What the hell is even going on here?* she thought, squeezing Finn's arm tighter. All she'd done was have a few drinks, talk Finn through his relationship drama, then have maybe a few *more* drinks. Nothing that should have landed her on an impromptu catwalk with an audience.

"It's the alcohol," she whispered to herself, forgetting that Finn could hear her.

"What's the alcohol?" He dipped his head, leaning closer to hear her.

"Everything," Lucy whispered again. "The drinks made me do it."

Finn nodded and lifted his free hand to wave at Elise, who was sitting on the arm of the couch, trying to position herself as close to Bradford Melton as possible. She winked at them and gave a little wave with her fingers.

"The drinks make us do crazy things," Finn agreed. "Which is why we should probably have another one."

Before Lucy could say no, she had another flute of champagne in her hand. And then another. And then finally—

She lost track. Of everything.

9

MARCH 19

ST. BARTS

F inn woke up feeling as if the entire world was an ocean beneath him. He opened his left eye, then his right: too bright. He shut them tightly and felt something scratching against his bare arm. Rather than opening his eyes to assess the situation, he rolled over on his side and fell back to sleep.

10

MARCH 19
ST. BARTS

Lucy woke up in a bright, unfamiliar room with the unsettling feeling that she'd had *far* too much to drink and, more importantly, that she might not be alone. She rolled over and sat up as slowly as possible, taking in each individual brain throb as it pounded against her skull. She deserved this, as well as the hangover that she'd most likely wrestle with all day long.

Once in a sitting position, Lucy blinked against the sunlight that streamed through the porthole window. *I'm not in my hotel room. I'm on a boat. I'm not even wearing my own clothes.* Lucy lifted the creamy tulle fabric in both hands and then let it go, watching it fall like crushed tissue paper around her thighs. *What the hell happened here?*

She scanned the room, looking for her sparkly purple purse and the dress she'd gone out in the night before, but as she slowly turned her pounding head a full 180 degrees, she saw nothing familiar. Nothing to indicate what had gone on, or even where she—

Oh god. Her head stopped moving. She gathered the skirt of the dress in her arms again as if it might protect her. Her eyelids fluttered. "Oh god," she whispered, shaking her head.

There was a man next to her. Asleep. On the bed.

"Hello," she said once, but it came out as a croak. Lucy cleared her throat and tried again. "Hello." She tapped the shoulder of the man gently as she scanned his body, which appeared to be fully clothed.

After a few more taps, he groaned and rolled over.

"Finn!" Lucy gathered the skirt of her dress and jumped to her feet—a move she regretted almost instantly. She dropped the skirt around her and pressed both hands against her temples to try to squash the monstrous headache pressing insistently against every inch of her skull.

Finn sat up, but he looked less surprised than Lucy felt. In fact, he looked almost curious.

"What happened? How is it morning?"

Lucy walked around the room in her bare feet, yanking up the bedskirt to look underneath for her purse and shoes. No luck.

"I don't know," Lucy said, turning in a full circle as the dress that Astrid had zipped her into the night before swished around her. "But I need to get out of here. We drank too much." She felt frantic. "I need to find my clothes and get back to the hotel."

Finn put his feet on the floor and groaned audibly as he sat up. "I feel like hell," he said, letting his head fall into his hands as he rested his elbows on his knees.

"I can't imagine that anyone would feel otherwise after how many frozen drinks we both had." Lucy felt the slightest chill of horror as she eyeballed Finn again, trying to determine whether they'd slept together. After that much alcohol, it seemed unlikely that either of them would have been able to close the deal.

"Okay," Finn sighed, standing up slowly. He was still partially hunched over when he went still. "Wait."

Lucy turned around again, as if her personal belongings might suddenly appear if she spun around enough times. "What? What's wrong?"

"I feel like we...like we might have..."

"What? Like we what?" Lucy could hear the wild panic in her own voice and she resisted the urge to jump across the bed and shake Finn. "What did we do?"

Finn stood the rest of the way up and looked Lucy in the eyes.

There was a long moment that felt suspended in amber as they stared at one another, searching, remembering.

There had been drinks, obviously. And Lucy walking (and with more alcohol, actually strutting) around the upper decks in the gown, letting people marvel at how well it fit her. The music had cranked up and given way to dancing. Moonlight—there had been plenty of moonlight.

Lucy opened her mouth to speak at the same time that Finn did.

"No," Lucy said, feeling a wave of dread and a wave of nausea crest inside of her at the same time.

"Lucy." Finn's eyes went wide. "I think..."

"No," Lucy said again, shaking her head. "No, it's just a dress. Nothing happened." She put her hands over her ears as if blocking out Finn's voice might make everything disappear.

"Lucy, I think we got married."

THE SHOWER LUCY TOOK WHEN SHE GOT BACK TO THE HOTEL ROOM WAS long and hot. She'd walked across the lobby in the rumpled cream dress she'd worn out the night before, her purse tucked under one arm, chin near her chest as she tried not to make eye contact with anyone.

Unfortunately, Alvin the concierge spotted her and came rushing over, hands clasped in front of him as he greeted her.

"Lucy!" he said, a huge smile on his tanned face. "Good morning!"

Lucy winced. "Hi, Alvin."

Understanding washed over him. "Oh, let me get you a coffee. Cream and sugar?"

"I'm fine, Alvin," Lucy said, sliding her black shades on and glancing around furtively. "I just need to hurry upstairs and get dressed and then I'll come back down and talk about the plans for the day, if that's okay."

"Of course," Alvin said discreetly, touching her wrist lightly with his warm fingertips. "You head up and I'll send a tray of coffee right away."

Lucy smiled at him wanly. "That would be amazing. Thank you."

Standing on her balcony now with a fluffy white towel wrapped around her head and her white robe tied around her body, she sipped a cup of the strong coffee that someone had kindly slipped in and delivered on a silver tray as she'd showered. The water was crystal clear and calm as she watched yachts moving around regally, their sails bowed against the slight breeze.

The sheer horror of the situation was still hitting her in incremental doses. She'd gotten rip-roaring drunk—something she never did at home—and woken up married to someone who was essentially a total stranger. In response to this thought, she winced, squeezing her eyes shut to make the image of Finn's eyes staring at her across the bed go away.

She sat down on one of the chairs on her balcony and poured herself more coffee. First things first: she needed to get to Nick right away and check on him. If he was feeling well, she'd wait for him downstairs while he got ready, but if he was under the weather, she'd find out what he needed to be more comfortable.

After Nick, she needed to do serious damage control. She and Finn had tracked down her dress and purse, she'd changed, and they'd run into Elise stumbling out of Bradford's own giant stateroom.

"Good morning, you two," Elise had said slyly, the kitten heels of her slippers click-clacking on the wooden floor as she closed the door to Bradford's room behind her. She wore a silky caftan that drifted around her and a huge, knowing grin on her face. "You get any sleep in there, newlyweds?"

"Oh sweet Jesus!" Lucy had wailed. Finn took her hand and squeezed it tightly.

"That good, huh?" Elise wiggled her eyebrows.

"Listen. Elise. Can you tell us what happened last night?" Finn pleaded with her.

"Babydoll, by the stunned look on your blushing bride's face, I'd say the best sex of both of your lives happened last night." Elise gave a little cackle and clapped her hands together, putting them in front of her nose as she watched them playfully with twinkling eyes.

Great sex and a tragic hangover must look weirdly similar, Lucy thought to herself as she tried taking deep, cleansing breaths.

"We were wondering what happened *before* we went to bed," Finn clarified. "Like, how exactly did we end up married?"

Lucy's cleansing breaths sped up enough that they were inching toward hyperventilation territory. The full force of the situation was hitting her: she was married to a guest on the trip. She was married to a man nearly ten years her junior. She was married to a firefighter who lived across the country and to whom she wasn't even romantically attracted. *She was married.*

"Oh! Well, you two looked so damned gorgeous walking around up there together, and after a few more bottles of champagne went around, you asked the ship's captain to marry you."

"Is that even legal?" Lucy blinked and held her eyes closed for a count of three before opening them.

"Sure it is, honey," Elise said, her smile fading. "Wait, are you two having regrets about this? It's terribly romantic. Just wonderful. We were all so excited for you, finding love like this—"

"Elise, Elise," Finn said, holding one hand up to stop her. "I know your heart is in the right place, but this is definitely not something that either of us—and I mean sober us—would have wanted. We can assure you."

"Yeah, I would not have done this," Lucy confirmed. "And we need to *un*do it as quickly as possible."

Elise shrugged helplessly. "I don't know how to help you, honey. Getting married by a ship's captain is the same as getting married by a priest. It's a done deal."

With some quick goodbyes, Lucy and Finn had hurriedly found an Uber and gotten back to the hotel, then parted ways outside so as not to be seen walking into the lobby together in last night's clothes and with alcohol on their breath.

"Okay," Lucy said to herself out on the balcony, setting her coffee cup on the table. She stood up and unwound the towel from around her damp hair. "Time to fix this."

NICK OPENED THE DOOR TO HIS ROOM AND SMILED AT LUCY. "HI," HE said, motioning for her to enter. He was wearing a pair of shorts, a loose-fitting button-up shirt with the sleeves rolled to his elbows, and a pair of tortoise-shell reading glasses. He held a book in his hand.

"How are you feeling?" Lucy looked at him closely. He seemed a million times better than he had the night before when he'd insisted on going directly back to his room after an early dinner.

"You know, it was a rough evening, but I'd say I'm at 80 percent. Can't complain."

"Food poisoning?"

"Could be, but it's behind me now," Nick said, closing the lid of his laptop on the coffee table. "I was just trying to read and write a little here until I heard from you. I'm sort of stuck with this new book I'm working on," he said, nodding toward his laptop. He finally took a good look at her and his face fell. "Yikes. What happened? Food poisoning for you as well?"

"More like alcohol poisoning." Lucy stuck her finger into her mouth like she was going to gag herself, but instead she just rolled her eyes theatrically. "Poor choices all evening, you know?"

"Been there." Nick shoved his hands into his pockets and looked around the room. "So what's the plan for today, Miss Landish?"

"I thought we should probably grab some breakfast, and then there's a day trip planned to the little village of St. Jean. It's got all these cute boutiques and restaurants and shops along the most crystal blue water you can imagine." Lucy tried to sound excited, but anxiety coursed through her. *She was married.*

"Shopping sounds *divine*," Nick said with an overdone British accent. "But seriously, I'm happy to go along and hold your bags if you want."

"There's a natural coral reef there and great swimming, so

honestly, if you felt like checking out the beach while I shop, then I wouldn't blame you one bit."

Nick shrugged and took off his glasses, setting them on the coffee table next to his laptop. "I'm game."

Breakfast was on a patio where waiters served fresh-squeezed juice, crisp bacon, poached eggs on thick slices of French bread, and a cup of tart, sweet fruit to guests in caftans, golf shorts, and sunglasses. Every bite of food fortified Lucy and brought her back to life—not to mention the fact that it helped to settle her stomach.

"More coffee?" Alvin asked, materializing next to their table with a porcelain carafe.

"It's like you read my mind." Nick smiled at the concierge. "Thank you."

Alvin put his hands behind his back and clasped his hands together, looking at them expectantly. "I hear congratulations are in order," he said, looking like he was ready to burst at the seams.

Nick frowned. "Sorry?"

Lucy's head snapped up and she looked directly at Alvin, silently begging him to say no more. But the runaway train of Alvin's words had been set in motion, and it was speeding toward Lucy as she stood on the tracks, eyes wide and legs unmoving.

"Alvin!" she shouted too loudly, standing up and nearly knocking over her chair in the process. She dropped her napkin on her empty chair. "I'd love to go over the next few excursions again with you really quickly so that I know when the vans will be here to pick people up. Is that okay?"

Alvin looked confused, but he nodded efficiently and backed away from the table. "Of course. I'm happy to go over everything with you."

Lucy held up a finger to Nick to let him know she'd be just a minute, and then followed Alvin to the front desk.

"So, listen," Lucy said in a hiss-whisper, leaning across the counter. Alvin's eyebrows shot up in alarm as he took in the crazed look on her face. "I need your help, Alvin."

"Yes, with the arrangements. I know—"

"No," Lucy said urgently, reaching across the counter and grabbing Alvin's wrist. He looked down at her hand in surprise and Lucy immediately realized that grabbing the concierge was taking things a step too far. She let go. "Sorry," Lucy said, holding both of her hands up in surrender. "It's just...I've gotten myself into a bit of a bind and I need some advice."

Alvin waited.

"Last night, I got married." She said the words and then waited for the gravity of the situation to hit him like a ton of bricks. From the still-expectant look on Alvin's face, she could tell that it had not hit him hard enough. "I got married and I *do not want to be married*."

"But you and your gentleman are such a lovely couple," Alvin said meekly, waving a hand in Nick's general direction. They both looked over at him on the patio, at sweet, wonderful Nick with his elbows on the table and his gaze cast out at the water as he sipped a cup of coffee.

"It's not him, Alvin. I married a stranger." Lucy felt a strangling sensation in her throat as the words came out. "I married one of the guests who came on this trip with my travel agency."

"Ohhhh," Alvin said, his mouth puckered and his forehead knit into a frown. He looked as pained as if he'd just had the misfortune of watching someone slip and fall dramatically in a public place. "That was an interesting choice."

"That was a *drunk* choice," Lucy said, willing herself to stay calm. "We got married on a yacht by the ship's captain, and now I need to know how to undo it. Immediately." She turned and shot Nick another glance over her shoulder. "Without him knowing."

"I see." Alvin stroked his chin like he had a thick, manly, well-groomed beard rather than a smooth jaw and a babyface. After pondering the situation for a moment, he held up both hands like a crossing guard. "Here's what I think you should do." He leaned across the counter so that his face was just inches from Lucy's. "I think you should finish breakfast and go about your day like the whole thing never happened."

Lucy's disappointment felt like a rock in the pit of her stomach.

"But that won't fix it," she said, tasting bile in her throat. "I'm sure the other party would also wish to cancel this as soon as possible, so if it means that we both have to be present, or if it's going to cost us some money to grease a few palms...whatever it is, we can do it."

"Lucy," Alvin said slowly, staring directly into her eyes. "You can go about your day and your life. This is not a legally binding marriage, so in effect, it never happened."

"What? How is that possible? A ship's captain married us. It has all the authority of a priest," she argued.

"Ah, but only if the captain really *is* a priest. Or a notary or some otherwise ordained official. If all he does is steer a ship, then you're probably okay."

"So, wait a second." Lucy stood up straighter, putting both palms flat on the front counter. "You mean to tell me all this time I've believed a ship's captain could legally marry someone? Is that just a myth? Or did we all watch too much *Love Boat*? I don't understand."

Alvin looked flummoxed. "I don't know for sure, but it's a commonly held notion, yes. I probably tell two or three people a year that they're fine after a night of too much champagne and not enough common sense. This happens, Lucy. Don't let it ruin your trip."

Well. This changes everything, Lucy thought. She exhaled and realized she'd been holding her breath tightly in her chest. "So no papers filed? No official record?"

"Not unless you go and file the papers yourself. I think you can pretty safely just assume that everyone on the yacht was having as much fun as you and that no one there took the marriage too seriously."

Lucy felt a laugh of pure relief escape her, and she put both hands to her chest. "Oh my god. Alvin, thank you. You have no idea how worried I was."

Alvin shrugged. "Again, it happens. Vacation, you know?"

Lucy raised her eyebrows and tipped her head from side to side, but deep down she knew that this was a reckless transgression that should have never happened. After all, what would the rest of the travel group think of her if they found out she'd married one of the other travelers? What kind of Yelp review would she get if they knew about *that*?

"Okay," Lucy said, stepping back from the counter. "Then I'm going to just go about the day, like you said."

"Great idea."

"Thanks again, Alvin."

"It's what I'm here for." Alvin bowed his head slightly and watched as Lucy walked back over to the patio to sit with Nick.

"All squared away?" Nick asked, signing the receipt with his room number and then closing the black leather book that held the bill.

"Completely," Lucy said, feeling a hundred pounds lighter than she had when she'd woken up that morning. *More like a hundred and seventy-five pounds lighter,* she thought, imagining Finn and trying to guess his weight. She sighed deeply again, letting her shoulders relax as she stood up with Nick and headed for the vans that were already waiting out front.

11

MARCH 19
ST. BARTS

The beach at St. Jean was totally accessible for families to just jump in and bob in the water as planes flew overhead. The sand was like powdered sugar and the water was a chlorinated blue, and all along the crescent of beach people sprawled comfortably while kids made sandcastles or chased each other around.

Jutting out from the shoreline like a pier was a circular hunk of land that held various shops and restaurants. To get to the red-roofed shops, pedestrians had to cross a small footbridge. The whole place had the feeling of a magical little beach village.

The vans let everyone out on the main street and Lucy stood on the sidewalk, counting heads like a teacher taking her students on a field trip.

"We'll meet back here at four o'clock," Lucy said, glancing at her watch and waiting as everyone scattered in different directions, some headed for the beach and others toward the shops. She turned to Nick, holding both wooden handles of her woven purse in her hands. "So, what should we do?"

Nick looked up and down the street. "I guess we should go and see what's on offer at the shops, huh? Maybe pick up a few souvenirs while we're here."

"You gonna get your mom a magnet or something?" Lucy walked next to Nick as they crossed over the footbridge. Beyond the tiny island of shops they could see people floating in the clear water, faces turned up to the warm sun, eyes closed as they drifted blissfully.

"Actually, she collects those little tiny spoons that you display on a wooden shelf. She's already got all fifty states, but I'm thinking she needs a St. Barts spoon."

Lucy slowed to a stop and whacked his arm with the back of her hand. "Shut up! My aunt Sharon has those spoons. When I went to Pennsylvania for my eighth grade trip she made me get her one. It had The Liberty Bell carved on the handle. Hey, what do you think they'd put on a St. Barts spoon?"

Nick considered this as they started walking again. "Hmmm. Maybe a girl in a bikini?"

"Your mom will love that."

"I'm kidding, by the way. My mom doesn't collect the spoons, but my grandma did and we inherited them when she died. I'm pretty sure they're in my parents' attic. But I do need to get something for Krista as a thank you for minding the shop for me while I'm away."

"Oooh, let's find her something here!" Lucy said, feeling renewed now that they had something to focus on. Her morning had already been full and she was running on low sleep and a hangover, but the fact that the wedding ceremony she'd participated in the night before had meant nothing was such a huge relief that she could easily forget both of those things and just have fun with Nick.

They started at the first shop on the little island, roaming through stacks of t-shirts, St. Barts collectibles, and shell jewelry. Lucy wrinkled her nose at him and gave a slight shake of the head. Living in Florida, they already had full access to this kind of ticky-tacky beach paraphernalia.

The next shop was filled with hats and bags woven from palm fronds. The woman behind the counter explained that the locals in one of the quarters of St. Barts made these items, and Nick picked out an oversized clutch purse that had rows of gold sequins woven in between the fronds. It was incredibly chic, and even though Lucy had never met Krista, she could imagine that it would go over well with his sister.

"Good choice," Lucy said, nodding in approval. She gave him a thumbs-up.

As they worked their way through the shops Lucy picked up a black Tahitian pearl on a leather cord that she had Nick tie on right away. She fingered the choker appreciatively as she looked into a small mirror in the shop, admiring the way the uneven shape of the pearl nestled into the dip between her clavicles.

"It's perfect," he said, watching her in the mirror from over her shoulder. Lucy looked up and caught his eye in the reflection.

"It's *imperfect*, and I love that," she countered.

Nick bought a bottle of rum, a loose, silky Hawaiian-type shirt printed with watercolor images of a regatta for his dad, and a seafood cookbook for his mom. Lucy picked up a cuff made of black leather that was inlaid with a chunk of rough, turquoise jasper stone.

"For Dev?" Nick asked simply, appearing at Lucy's elbow as she turned the bracelet back and forth and looked at the price tag.

She lifted one shoulder. "Well, I thought it would be nice of us to bring him back a gift."

"Us?" Nick snorted. "I think he'd rather get a gift from you."

Lucy rolled her eyes. "Whatever. I just think it's nice to bring home souvenirs. I got these for my aunt Sharon, who is looking after my mom," she said, opening her hand to reveal a pair of bottle green sea glass earrings. "And I'm looking at a hand-painted shirt for my mom," she added, lifting her chin toward an oversized blouse on a mannequin. It was covered with bright pastels and belted with a brown leather cord. Even though her mother refused to leave the house, Lucy felt like she could still bring a little of the world home to her mom.

"Those are thoughtful presents," Nick said, eyeing the shirt on the mannequin. "But I'm starting to get all shopped out. Do you think it's too early for us to make our purchases and go sit on a patio for an afternoon drink and an appetizer?"

Lucy looked up from the earrings in her palm. "You're already hungry?"

Nick made a guilty face. "I think it's all the sea air. I wake up ravenous and then spend the whole day looking for my next meal."

"Well, we do live at the beach at home, but let's definitely blame it on the sea air." Lucy winked at him and went to pay for all of her finds.

They chose a table at the railing inside a little bar with a patio that looked right out onto the aquamarine Caribbean Sea. Nick ordered a handmade pizza with tomato, mozzarella, arugula, and prosciutto to share, and without hesitation, Lucy ordered a *piscine*, which was just a glass of rosé with a few cubes of ice.

Nick lifted one eyebrow as she ordered her drink. "A little hair of the dog?"

"God yes," she said, laughing as she handed the menu over to the waiter.

They could feel the breeze coming off the water as a three man band with steel drums started to play nearby, the sounds wafting all around as the waiter dropped off their drinks.

"So," Nick said, lifting his beer. "To another day in paradise, and to not feeling sick today." He winced. "Sorry—I should have said *I* feel better today, but I'm sorry you're not quite yourself."

"Nothing to worry about at all," Lucy promised, taking the first sip of her drink. She was about to say something else when a flash of fiery red hair and a loud laugh caught her attention. It was Elise, dressed in a flowing shift and large enamel bangles on each wrist. She was leading two of the other women from the trip over to a table about thirty feet away, and for a second Lucy hoped that the women might not spot them.

"Oh! You guys!" Elise waved a hand high in the air and said something to the other ladies before weaving through the tables and chairs to greet Nick and Lucy. "Sorry we missed the van ride over. It took us a little longer to get ready this morning, so we caught our own ride. You know how it is," she said, turning to Nick with a wink, "ladies of a certain age need more time to put on our faces."

"Well, you look lovely to me," Nick said, smiling up at her. That was the thing Lucy loved about Nick: he was amazingly sincere with everyone he met. His ability to flatter and find kind words for everyone who entered his shop back home made him an Amelia Island favorite.

Elise put a hand on Nick's shoulder and squeezed as she laughed. "You're a doll. But you know," she said, lowering her voice, "you *are* out on the town with a married woman."

The smile died on Nick's face as he glanced back at Lucy with a look of confusion. "No, Lucy's divorced," he said, settling in his own mind on the fact that Elise must be confused.

"I'm definitely single," Lucy interjected, scooting back in her chair and standing up abruptly. "Any idea where the ladies' room is?" She looked around wildly.

"I think it's back there, honey," Elise said, pointing a long red nail towards a hallway near the kitchen.

"Come with me." Lucy grabbed onto Elise's forearm and pulled her along, not giving her a chance to say another word. "Be right back," she called to Nick, already walking away.

"Honey," Elise said, scampering along behind Lucy in her kitten-heeled sandals. "Slow down. Where's the fire?"

As soon as they were on the other side of the swinging door of the restroom, Lucy bent forward at the waist and peered under the stalls. No feet.

"Listen," she hissed, looking at Elise as if what she were about to say was deadly serious. "I got things cleared up and Nick *cannot hear* about what happened last night."

Elise frowned and pulled her arm away from Lucy's grasp, rubbing it gently with the other hand like she'd been bruised. "Why not? He's not your boyfriend, is he?"

"Well, no, he's not," Lucy said, taking a deep breath. "But there is something there. I just don't know what exactly. When we're at home, it's like...there's a flirtation. A current between us. And the other night we were out walking—"

The door swung open and a woman holding the hand of a little girl in a red polka dotted sundress walked in. She smiled at Lucy and Elise and then closed the door to the oversized handicapped stall so that she and her daughter could be in there together.

"Anyway," Lucy went on, taking a step closer to Elise. "I think it could really be something. And the other night when Nick wasn't feeling well, I went out on my own and ran into Finn, and that was all a huge mistake. We need to pretend that never happened."

"So are you getting it annulled?" Elise asked loudly, still looking confused.

Lucy put a finger to her lips and dropped her voice. "No need to get an annulment," she whispered. "I talked to the concierge at the hotel and he assured me that a ship's captain has no real authority to marry anyone. It's not binding."

"Are you sure, honey? Because I swear Captain Stubing married at least a few guests on *The Love Boat*..."

"There was also an episode where a chimpanzee wore dresses and stole from everyone's staterooms," Lucy said with more than just a touch of sarcasm.

"Touché." Elise walked over to the mirror, her heels click-clacking on the marble tile. She leaned in and touched the tip of her ring finger to her lips, then swiped a tube of lipstick from her purse over both full lips. "So if it was all just a big hoax, then what's the fuss? Nick seems like the kind of guy who could have a laugh about something like that."

Lucy thought about it. "I guess he might be." She moved to the mirror next to Elise's and eyed her own reflection: auburn hair washed but not dried; her usual tan with the brush of freckles across her slender nose; green eyes, gold hoop earrings, peach lip gloss. She turned her head and looked at Elise. "I don't know if I want to find out though. If he ends up thinking I'm a nut or a drunk or just totally impulsive, then he might write me off completely. I'm honestly none of those things. In fact, until I moved to Florida, I would have said I had a good head on my shoulders and an excess of common sense."

Elise snapped her purse shut and tucked it under one arm. "Or he might think you're charming, fun-loving, and the kind of girl who takes chances."

With a sigh, Lucy nodded. "Still. Can we not tell him?"

Elise patted Lucy's arm and walked over to the door with a resigned smile. "Sure, honey. Whatever you think is best."

Back on the patio, Elise went to join the other women at her table, and Lucy sat with Nick, watching his face as he ate pizza with abandon. It was amazing to her that just the night before he'd been sick enough to stay in, but here he was now, eating and drinking like it had never happened. If only it really *hadn't* happened, then she wouldn't have gotten completely smashed, and she would never have agreed to put on a frou-frou wedding dress and sashay around like some idiot, and she absolutely positively would *not* have married Finn in a drunken ceremony that she didn't even remember.

"What are you thinking about?" Nick grinned at her as he tore off another slice of pizza, folded it in half, and took a big bite.

Lucy shook her head, trying to banish all thoughts of the night before. Certainly it wasn't Nick's fault that he hadn't felt well; it wasn't his responsibility to keep her in check. "I'm just thinking about how glad I am that you're here."

A look of happiness washed over Nick's face. "Really? I'm glad I'm here too. It beats the hell out of Dev giving me decaf when I order regular and out of Honey refusing to give me a French manicure no matter how much I offer to pay."

"Oh god!" Lucy's hands flew to her face. "I totally forgot—I can't believe I forgot to tell you this!"

Nick lowered the pizza and looked at her with mild alarm in his eyes. "What?"

"I got a text from Dev last night."

"Ugh." Nick gave a mock eye roll that was most definitely not totally an act.

"No, it was about Honey."

Now Nick looked worried. "Just tell me," he said, his pitch rising alongside his level of concern.

"Her shop got robbed. They broke the window and smashed things up, but everyone is fine. And they only hit her store."

"No way," Nick said, letting the piece of pizza he'd been eating with such gusto just a moment before flop onto his plate. "What the hell..."

"I know. I was so stunned and I totally forgot to even respond to him. I should do that now."

"Yeah," Nick said, casting his eyes out at the water. "Krista didn't even text me. I had no idea."

"I'm sure she didn't want to worry you since nothing happened to The Carrier Pigeon."

"I guess." He looked uncomfortable as he took in the news of the robbery. "Poor Honey though."

Lucy had her phone in her hand and she'd opened the text and clicked on the photo from Dev. "He sent this."

Nick glanced at the picture and then turned away as if she'd shown him an image of a severed head on a stake. He made a strangled sound. "No, that's terrible. Running a business is such hard work, and to think that someone could just trash it like that. I can't."

"I hear you," Lucy said, nodding firmly. She closed the photo and tapped out a quick response to Dev, hit send, and then locked her phone and put it away. "I'm just glad she's okay."

Nick pushed the pizza away; a pall had been cast over his hearty appetite and easygoing mood. "Want to walk around some more?"

Lucy drained her *piscine* in one gulp and nodded as she waved at their waiter to ask for the check. "Yes. I do."

THAT NIGHT, A SHARP PAIN IN LUCY'S SIDE WOKE HER IN THE DARK. SHE shot up in her bed, hand flying to her ribcage, face contorted in pain. With several deep, cleansing breaths, she got the ache to subside enough to swing her legs around and put her feet on the floor. She reached for her phone and texted Nick.

Are you awake?

She waited for a response. Of course he wasn't awake at three o'clock in the morning. Lucy locked her phone and set it on the nightstand.

The windows that looked out over the balcony were covered with a curtain that she pulled back, wincing in pain as she did. She unlocked the sliding door and opened it, stepping out onto the cool tile and feeling the night on her skin.

Mercifully, the pain ebbed away, leaving a hollow feeling in Lucy's chest. She sat on one of the chairs and put her bare feet up on the table, watching as the stars blinked above the water and the earth. It didn't happen often, this sort of middle-of-the-night panic attack that left her with a sharp pain or gasping for breath, but occasionally she woke up after midnight with a cry or a start, as if she'd just realized how truly alone in the world she was.

Lucy rested the back of her head against the chair and looked out at the sky. As she did, hot tears spilled from the corners of her eyes, running down her temples and into her hair. It wasn't loneliness, per se, but the particular reckoning a person did every so often with the very fact of being alone. She reached up and wiped the tears from her skin with the back of her hands and stood up. Sitting here at three o'clock in the morning feeling sorry for herself wasn't going to get her anywhere. Going back to bed wasn't going to get her anywhere either, as she felt the last vestiges of sleep recede and leave behind a wakefulness that grew under the light of the moon.

Wearing a white satin robe that was open to reveal her navy blue men's pajamas and a pair of matching white satin slippers, Lucy padded through the hallway to the elevator, punched the button, and rode down to the lobby.

There was no one behind the front desk, and the lights were turned down low. Out on the pool deck Lucy counted three heads: a woman sitting on the side of a lounge chair, facing a man as they talked quietly, and closer to the water, a man whose laptop screen glowed in the dark night. Lucy followed the light of the screen like it was a beacon.

As she got closer, she realized what she felt she'd known all along: the man with the laptop was Nick.

"Hey," she said, stopping next to him. Her robe swished around her.

Nick looked up in surprise. "Hey yourself," he said, setting his laptop at the foot of the lounge chair and turning to look up at her. "What are you doing awake?"

Lucy glanced at his computer screen: a word doc. He was clearly up and working on his latest novel, which was something she knew he did when he couldn't sleep. The palm fronds around the pool shimmied slightly as a hint of a breeze picked up off the water.

"I woke up and had that feeling."

Nick patted the cushion of his chair and scooted over so that Lucy could sit next to him. "The one that feels like a panic attack?" He put one arm in the air so she could slide under it, then he wrapped it around her shoulders as she settled in.

"It kind of does. I used to get it more when I first realized that I was an adult and there was no one but me to take care of myself and my mom."

Nick chuckled lightly and looked at the pool, lit from beneath the water with warm yellow lights. "I'm not laughing at you, by the way," he clarified, turning his head so that his face was closer to hers. "I'm just relating to that feeling you get when it hits you like a ton of bricks that there's no safety net, you know? I remember the first time it really caught up to me. I was about twenty-eight and my dad had just died, and I looked at my mom and thought, 'The woman is only in her mid-fifties, but she looks utterly lost. How will she survive another thirty or forty years on her own?'"

Lucy nodded knowingly. "How long was it until she got her feet under her again?"

"Honestly, I'm not sure she ever fully did," Nick admitted. "I mean, she got married again and she seems reasonably happy, but I

think losing someone unexpectedly takes away the last of your inno-
cence. And I'm speaking of both my mom and myself here."

"Being an adult is hard," Lucy said, turning to look him in the eye.
"And I'm not just saying that."

Nick smiled gently. "No, I know you're not just saying it. It isn't for
the faint of heart."

Lucy took a deep breath. Buoyed by the darkness and the
soothing tranquility of the pool with its low underwater lights, she
forced herself to speak. "I did something stupid last night, but I didn't
want to tell you about it because I thought it might make things weird
between us."

Nick stayed quiet, waiting.

"Last night when you weren't feeling well, I went to the owner's
reception on the yacht of Elise's new man friend, just like I told you."

"Okay," Nick said, sounding completely neutral; interested, but
not in any way concerned.

"And I drank too much." Lucy stopped there, wondering if this
alone might satisfy her urge to be honest with him. It didn't, so she
went on. "And there was this weird lady there who designs wedding
dresses. Ingrid something or other, and she talked me into putting on
one of her gowns."

Nick nodded and looked at the pool. "I bet you looked gorgeous."

"I bet I looked drunk and stupid," Lucy said, leaning into him and
hoping that the closeness would make the story sound more like a
funny anecdote than a dumb mistake. "But the worst part was that I
woke up this morning and I was married."

Nick pulled away from her slightly. Lucy kept her eyes fixed on
the swimming pool and the way the water remained placid and calm
without any swimmers.

"Married? To some rich guy who owns a yacht?" An inkling of
judgment crept into Nick's voice. "Wow."

"No." Lucy sat up and turned her body towards Nick so that they
were facing each other. The arm he'd had around her shoulders fell
to his side. "Apparently—though I remember none of it, which is
embarrassing enough—I got married to Finn."

"Finn," Nick said, lowering his chin as he stared at her. "The kid from California—that Finn?"

Lucy shrugged. "Yes. That Finn. And he's only like ten years younger than us, which I'm not sure qualifies as a 'kid.'"

"Huh." Nick finally looked away from her face, focusing his eyes on the palm fronds that moved against the dark sky, lit from below by lights fixed at the base of the tree trunks. "Finn."

"But listen—"

"You don't need to explain," Nick said, holding up both hands. "Really."

"No, I do." Lucy reached out and took his right hand, pulling it into her lap and holding it. "Nothing happened. Less than nothing. We drank, I'm sure we walked around the yacht like dummies, acting stupid and showing off the wedding gown, and then somebody had the great idea of having the ship's captain marry us, though I'm not sure who exactly I have to thank for that."

"Lucy," Nick said, shaking his head and sounding mildly uncomfortable.

"We woke up next to one another in the stateroom, but I promise you that *nothing* happened. Nothing at all. And we were both completely horrified. Oh," she said, remembering the most important part, "and I talked to Alvin at the concierge desk this morning first thing, and he assured me that a ship's captain has no real authority to marry people, so it was just basically some stupid joke."

Nick stayed quiet for a long minute. He looked like he was thinking, though Lucy had no idea what might be going through his mind. "Why were you so afraid to tell me that? Was that what Elise was referring to today when she said I was out with a married woman?"

Lucy's eyes fell to her lap and she suddenly grew very interested in a hang nail on her thumb. She nodded. "Yeah. I just didn't want to tell you because it made me seem flighty. I'm not really the type to drink and do regrettable things."

"Hey, it happens. Any other reason?"

Lucy picked at the nail of one thumb with the nail of the other for a second. "I thought...I kind of thought we were having a moment the other night, and I just didn't want you to get the wrong idea." She blew out a loud exhale. "I didn't want you to think I'd kissed Finn or anything crazy."

It was Nick's turn to take her hand in his and hold it. Lucy looked up and noticed that the other couple on the pool deck had gone in, leaving them entirely alone, though she could now see a woman sitting behind the front desk inside the lobby, and two tired looking men in the breakfast area, moving slowly as they set up tables and chairs.

"Okay," Nick said softly. "I'm going to tell you something." He waited until she was looking at his eyes. "I don't tell many people this, but I want you to understand that we all have secrets. We have things that we're either not proud of, or we just don't like to share, and that's actually okay. It's fine. What happened last night—while sure, maybe a little flighty—hurt no one, right?"

Lucy nodded, acquiescing.

"But as for me, the thing I don't like to share isn't something that makes me look flighty. It's something serious and it's something that I hold close to my heart. But I want you to know that you telling me your secret means I feel comfortable telling you mine." Nick paused and swallowed. "When I was in college, I was dating a girl named Laura. She got pregnant when we were twenty-one."

Lucy inhaled slowly, trying to keep her eyes from growing wide. Nick had a child? Or, at the very least, he'd gotten someone pregnant nearly twenty years ago?

He squeezed her hand and went on. "Laura and I had a little girl we named Daisy, and while it was far sooner in life than either of us had planned as far as becoming parents, we were completely smitten with her. We didn't marry, and we didn't even pretend that that was on the radar. Our only jobs were finishing school and raising Daisy, and we were doing okay at both things, considering our youthfulness and lack of material resources." Nick's eyes fell to the hand that held Lucy's and he stopped talking for a minute. "When Daisy was one, she had her first seizure."

Lucy drew in a sharp breath, unable to hide her shock this time. "No," she whispered.

Nick nodded and chewed on his bottom lip. "Yeah, and it wasn't good. We had some tests done, and it turned out that she had retinoblastoma, which is a cancer of the eye. The seizures happened more frequently, and we found out that it had spread to her brain."

Without warning, Lucy's eyes filled with tears. "Oh, Nick," she said softly. "I'm so sorry." He didn't even have to go on for her to know how this story ended.

"She died just before her second birthday. It was fast and merciless, and a part of me never recovered from it. I know Laura didn't fully recover either. We stayed together another six months, but that was all we could take. The constant reminders were too much." He sat up straighter and looked at the palm trees again. "I didn't tell you so that you'd feel sorry for me or anything, Lucy. I just wanted you to know that we all have episodes of our lives—big ones and small ones —that we pack up and put away, and we aren't obligated to share them with the world."

Lucy's head bobbed in acknowledgment. "I hear you. And thank you. Thank you for sharing and thank you for understanding. You really have a way with words." She sniffed a little and wiped at her nose with the back of her hand. Hearing about Daisy had really shaken her.

"Hey, that's why they pay me the big bucks, you know? I use my fancy words to create the world's most engaging mystery novels and I'm *clearly* reaping the financial rewards," he scoffed, pulling her arm so that she turned around and faced the pool again, sliding in next to him as she had before their talk.

"Oh, I know that," Lucy assured him. "I never doubted for a minute that you were only using The Carrier Pigeon as a front to hide the fact that you're a multi-millionaire and a famous, sexy author."

"And also as an excuse to play with a fax machine all day," Nick added as he reached over and pinched Lucy's thigh. "Now, I have a big problem."

"What is it?"

Nick reached for his laptop, which was still on the foot of the lounge chair. He touched the trackpad and the screen came back to life. "I'm a little bit stuck on this scene, and I'd like to go to bed before the sun comes up. Do you think you could help me?"

"I *do* know a lot of dark stuff, so I might be able to help you write your mystery," Lucy said, relaxing into his side as she focused her eyes on the computer screen. "Do you need to know anything about dead bodies?"

"You know," Nick said, already deep in thought. "It's slightly incongruous with our surroundings," he swept a hand across the still, tropical pool deck and the clear night sky, "but I could throw in a dead body or two. Let's talk."

And with a project between them to change the topic, Lucy and Nick were able to put all of the ugly, regrettable, sad, unfortunate parts of their pasts back where they belonged and laugh about the hapless detective in Nick's latest mystery novel. Neither one of them went back to bed or got any more sleep, but in Lucy's mind, it was the perfect way to end one day and start another.

12

MARCH 20

ST. BARTS

Elise was in heaven. Bradford was everything she'd been hoping for: successful; her age; attentive; funny. And he really seemed to like her. She'd woken up that morning to find a dozen roses being wheeled in on a breakfast cart, and while he was going to be out at the regatta all day, he'd left her explicit instructions to get a massage or a facial and to charge it all to his room.

Feeling much less groggy than she had the first time she'd woken up in his room, Elise nearly hopped out of bed and threw on the dress she'd been wearing the night before, slipping her feet into her sandals and pulling her hair back with a clip that she'd left on the bathroom counter. With Bradford gone for the day, she only had so many hours to get herself ready to see him again, and on top of that, she had a bit of detective work to do.

In the lobby, Elise made a beeline for the front desk. "Good morning," she said to the woman who was tapping on the keyboard of a computer and wearing a name tag that said Celine. "I was hoping you might be able to help me."

Celine's fingers stopped moving and she gave Elise a measured, professional smile. "Yes, of course. How can I help, ma'am?"

"I'm staying with Bradford Melton," she said, leaning into the desk so that she could lower her voice, "and I was hoping to reach out to his adult children back home and start to plan a surprise party for when we get home. Do you think you could give me some of the information you have on file? Maybe an emergency contact?" She had lain in bed for a bit that morning, already imagining that he would have put his daughter Michelle, whom he'd told her all about, down as an emergency contact. After all, wasn't that what grown daughters were for?

Celine gave Elise a long, lingering look that made her feel as if she'd shown up to the front desk naked instead of simply in her wrinkled dress from the night before and not wearing any makeup.

"Well," Celine said, clearly weighing the happiness that a surprise birthday party might bring to an important guest like Bradford against the breach of policy she'd be committing by giving a disheveled woman his personal information. Her face betrayed the slightest distaste at Elise's appearance before she turned back to her computer. "Okay. I guess I can see what we have on file."

"Thank you, honey," Elise said, setting her purse on the counter and lacing her fingers together as she rested on her elbows and waited. She glanced around the lobby and took in the fresh flowers that were replaced daily, the way the marble floors shone in the morning light, and the studied glamour of the women already dressed in tennis whites and pool cover-ups over expensive swimwear. She touched her hair in its clip and prayed to god that she wouldn't catch a glimpse of her puffy eyes or pale cheeks in the polished brass door of the elevator on the way to her own room.

"I really shouldn't do this," Celine said, her eyes flicking around the lobby as if someone might be watching. She took a pen and a notepad and scratched some information on the paper quickly, tearing it off and sliding it across the desk. "But here is his emergency contact information. It's Michelle Melton in Connecticut, and he's given this phone number and email address."

A warmth spread through Elise's body as she folded the paper in half and slipped it into her purse. She gave Celine a winning smile.

"Thank you so much. I know he's going to be surprised and he's going to love this."

Celine looked like she already regretted taking part in the whole thing. "Good. Great. Have a wonderful day." She was already back to her tap-tapping on the keyboard by the time Elise had turned and started the walk across the lobby—the Walk of Shame, as it was known, given that she was still in last night's smudged mascara and a dress that smelled of stale perfume and sweat, most likely looking like she'd been up to exactly what she *had* been up to. Maybe she should take up Bradford's offer after all and get a facial or something in the spa.

But no, she thought, pushing the button for the elevator three times as if that might make it move faster. *There will be plenty of time in the future to live like a queen.* The elevator dinged and the door opened, giving Elise the exact reflection of herself in the mirrored elevator that she'd hoped to avoid.

"Before anything," she said aloud to herself, alone in the elevator as the doors slid shut, "coffee and a shower."

DOUGLAS RITTENHOUR HAD BEEN THE LOVE OF HER LIFE, WITHOUT question. Elise had met Doug at a Fourth of July party in her best friend's backyard when she was twenty-one, and nothing had ever been the same. Doug was tall, owned his own small business, had a booming laugh, and was just as gregarious as she was. Together, they were the couple everyone wanted to invite to a party. Over the years they'd raised two daughters, opened three more businesses together, and traveled the world. His death had left a hole in Elise's life that no amount of lunches with friends, no cruises with her sister, no man could ever fill. Until now. It was just her luck that she'd met Bradford her first night on St. Barts, and that he was everything she'd been hoping for.

Mind you, there had been gentleman *friends* over the years; a woman of Elise's appetites needed companionship and someone to go out on the town with. She'd never liked sleeping alone, and over the twenty years since Doug's death, she'd taken vacations with other men, gone to concerts and plays, eaten at some fabulous restaurants —but she'd always been careful not to take anything too seriously. It wasn't until recently that she'd realized how much she needed a man. A good man. One with resources and connections. Like she'd told Lucy on the first night of this trip, a woman needed someone she could count on.

Elise walked through her hotel room in her robe, feeling clean and awake after her shower. She stood at the open windows that overlooked the balcony and held her shoulders back, head high. She felt regal. Having the interest of a man with Bradford's money, influence, and power made her feel somehow whole again. There had been times in her forties and fifties where she'd assumed that was all over for her; that no man with sex appeal or money would ever be interested in her again when he could have a woman half her age. And men could have that—make no mistake—there was never a shortage of young vixens ready to flaunt everything they had at a man with money. It was frustrating to watch women who still belonged in the shallow end of the pool do a swan dive into the deep end, sweep through the water like sharks, and scoop up all the floating men.

*But now...*Elise ran her hands over the heavy fabric of the curtains that hung floor-to-ceiling at the windows, feeling like a queen looking out over her kingdom. Now she had Bradford, and she'd do everything in her power to show him that she was what was missing from his life. Her years of party planning, dinner organizing, and family wrangling had served her well as she prepared for this next role, and now, for the first time, she felt ready to truly be with someone again. The memory of Doug was a happy one, but after twenty years, it was just that—a memory.

As she got ready for the day ahead, Elise thought of the times that her daughter had tried to talk to her about the future. There had been that weekend they'd spent together at a spa for Elise's sixtieth birthday, when Nina had brought up finances and life expectancy and how worried she got just thinking of her mother in old age, unable to afford proper care. As Elise had looked into her daughter's young, hopeful, unlined face, she'd wanted to reach out and slap her. Not to be cruel, but to wake her up. She wanted to shout: "You'll be old one day, too, you ripe, gorgeous girl! One day you'll be divorced or widowed and staring into the gaping hole of your own future, so don't *you* tell *me* what being old without means looks like!" But instead, she'd simply smiled at her beloved oldest child and given a single nod. "I know you worry about me, sweetheart, but you don't have to," she'd said instead.

After all, she worried about her own finances enough for the both of them. When Doug had passed away unexpectedly he'd left a life insurance policy, of course, but in the past twenty years, that had helped pay for her kids to go to college and had paid off the mortgage. There might have been a cruise or two with her sister, and a down payment on a late model Mercedes, but really, nothing crazy. The money had just vanished, as money is wont to do.

Over the years Elise had worked as an office manager and an executive assistant, but she was *tired*; the other women she knew who volunteered and took part in the community the way that she did were either retired, or happily ensconced in homes paid for by their wealthy husbands. She was ready to retire into the role of full-time wife and to focus on sumptuous meals, upcoming vacations, holidays. It was time to put her worries behind her.

Sitting in front of the lighted vanity mirror in the bathroom, Elise leaned in close and applied her eye makeup. She imagined Nina coordinating with Bradford's daughter Michelle to make sure that the wedding between their parents went off without a hitch. Maybe it would take place in a rose garden. Or on a beach. Maybe the children would stand up and give speeches about how happy they were for their parents. Certainly the ring would be substantial—not that Elise minded too much for carats when she was more worried about stability—and the honeymoon would be romantic. Perhaps they'd travel somewhere on Bradford's yacht. Or fly to the Maldives and rent one of those gorgeous huts that sit over the clear blue water.

Elise stood, blinked, examined her face, and deemed it worthy. Quickly, she dressed for the day and put the important things into her purse: room key, credit cards, phone, lipstick, the piece of paper with the information Celine had written for her at the front desk. There was no time to waste.

In the lobby, she was directed to a back room where three computers were available for guests to use. It was empty. Elise chose one, slipped on her reading glasses, and then sat and contemplated the desktop for just a moment: where to go? Which icon to click? Ah, Google Chrome—there it was. She opened her email and started a new message.

Hello, Michelle! I hope this message finds you well, and I hope this doesn't catch you unawares, but I know that we don't have much time to work with here. My name is Elise Rittenhour, and your father and I met in St. Barts. We've been spending quite a bit of time together, and oh my! He's a fabulous man, isn't he?

This might be terribly forward of me, but I'd really like to start planning a surprise birthday party for him, as I know his big day is just weeks away! I currently live in Texas, but I'll be flying in for the event, of course, and I'd love your help to get it underway. Can I count on you? Do you think he might like a big party, or a small one? Perhaps something with a yachting theme? I'm open to all suggestions at this point!

Please feel free to email me back any time—I'll be with your father a lot this week, so calling or texting would be more difficult.

Best wishes and I can't wait to meet you!

Sincerely,

Elise

With a satisfied smile, Elise re-read the email. It was perfect. Not too pushy, and it was clear that she was totally enamored of Bradford. She wanted Michelle to feel unthreatened, but also secure in the knowledge that her father had found a good, solid, capable woman. She hit send and then logged off. It was time to get out and enjoy the day.

13

MARCH 20

ST. BARTS

I t had gotten worse, his missing Carina. Finn hadn't slept much since the morning he'd woken up married to Lucy. In the end, it was kind of a funny story, but even as a single guy with no one to answer to, he'd been relieved that nothing had happened between them, as he still considered himself to be attached to Carina. But was he? No. He'd done everything she'd asked and he'd stepped away, to give her space. But he'd hated every second of it.

Now, as he wandered a busy street lined with shops and cafes, Finn walked slowly and without direction. The sun was high above, and he hadn't been able to bring himself to book that plane ticket home. Sure, getting back there and getting back to work sounded appealing in the broadest sense, but the reality of waking up in his bed alone, of not having evenings filled with Carina, of never coming home after work find that she'd opened a bottle of wine and roasted a chicken—those were things he couldn't bear.

Finn paused at a cafe and read the menu posted under glass: mahi mahi. Fresh grilled lobster. Chinese noodles with coconut milk. A lentil salad with crudités. None of it appealed to him and he walked on.

Would it be wrong to call her? Maybe just leave a message to say that he was getting on fine without her? A lie, of course, but a way to let her know that he'd been thinking of her while still honoring her wishes. After all, she'd never said no contact, she'd just urged him to move on. So yes, a phone call. No harm in a short, gentlemanly message wishing her well and letting her know she was on his mind.

Before he could stop himself, Finn had found a bench that looked out onto the street and opened up his contacts in his phone. He chose Carina. It rang.

Finn watched as cars passed by: Mini Coopers, Jeeps, Teslas. Mixed in were the boxy little beach rentals like the one he'd been driving. The phone rang three more times and went to voice mail.

He almost hung up, but just before punching the button to end the call, Finn put the phone back to his ear and searched for the words he wanted to say. Carina would already know he'd called just by the alert on her home screen, so saying nothing would be stupid and childish, and there was no way that Finn wanted to come across as stupid and childish.

"Hi," he finally said, exhaling. "I just wanted to call and say that I miss you. A lot. And that's not to make you feel bad," he hurried on, trying to get the message right. "I just do. I'm in St. Barts right now—alone—and it's beautiful here. Not as beautiful as you, but hey, how can turquoise water, sandy beaches, and multi-million dollar yachts compare with you on a Sunday morning?" Finn smiled to himself. "Anyway, some weird things have happened, and I just needed you to know that I'm thinking of you. That I'm trying to give you what you want, but, Carina—I'm still yours."

This last part escaped his mouth before Finn could stop it, and when the message cut off after "Carina—" he wasn't sure whether he felt annoyance or relief. She'd get the message (if she was even willing to listen) and hear that weird things happened, and that he'd said her name with a plea in his voice, but she wouldn't hear the words "I'm still yours." Finn locked his phone and stared at the black screen. Was it even a wise move? His buddies at the fire station would most likely give him a resounding, "Hell no!" and admonish him for the weak moment, but then they didn't know about Carina. For a brief moment he'd entertained the idea of telling the other guys at the station that he was in love with a woman twenty years his senior who had—oh, by the way—been his English teacher once upon a blue moon. That would be a doozy.

Finn looked at his phone screen: still dark, no return texts. But okay, he'd done it. He'd let her know that he wasn't over her. No regrets.

He stood and shoved his phone into the deep pocket of his cargo shorts, then walked back to the cafe with the menu outside. Maybe some fresh grilled lobster wouldn't be so bad after all. And maybe a beer, because why not? Who cared that it was only noon? Finn took a seat at a small table on the sidewalk and leaned back in his chair, ready to watch the world pass him by. Two teenage boys with long, muscled limbs crossed the street, one with a soccer ball tucked under his arm. An elderly woman wearing an expensive silk dress with a little dog on a leash smoked a cigarette as she spoke to a younger woman on the sidewalk. The sun glinted off of parked cars.

Maybe he'd ask Lucy out. That guy Nick was always around, but they didn't seem attached and while Finn wasn't necessarily interested in dating Lucy, they were both single, so why not? It would be like a first attempt to get out there again, but a safe one, since he and Lucy would never see each other again after this week. He could take her to watch the regatta, if she had time to break away from the group. Or maybe they could have dinner. After all, they were already married. He tried to laugh to himself about that little fact but couldn't.

A waiter set a sweaty glass of beer in front of Finn and as he nodded his thanks, he was already disregarding the whole idea. It wasn't that a woman ten years his senior might laugh him off; Carina was proof that he held appeal for an older woman. It was more that he couldn't help thinking that everything would all be just a little bit better if Carina was here with him, holding his hand as they shared an afternoon drink and watched the world go by.

THE HOLIDAY ADVENTURE CLUB GROUP HAD A SET TIME TO MEET IN the lobby to caravan to the vantage point for optimal regatta viewing. It wasn't so much that Finn was dying to see the yachts in action, but he'd eschewed all other activities so far in favor of just wandering aimlessly, so it seemed like a good idea to jump into an organized activity and stay focused. After all, if he was staying on St. Barts, then he might as well start to truly enjoy the island.

The lobby of the hotel was full of people he recognized from the group, including the sisters from Idaho who'd cornered him at dinner on the first night. They were funny and chatty and while Finn had enjoyed their company, he didn't necessarily want to be sandwiched between two grandmothers who smelled like perfume and hair spray for the whole day. And what was it with the older women trying to monopolize him? He glanced around, remembering Elise's flirtation on the airplane and the Idaho sisters taking turns touching his arm as they'd talked to him at dinner. Was it the firefighter thing? Or did every woman secretly harbor some desire to show a younger man what she'd learned over the years? He didn't want to flatter himself too much, but the feeling of being a desired object was real.

Instead of making any commitments for the regatta, Finn walked to the bar and ordered a bottle of water, then took out his phone and scrolled. Right away he spotted his outgoing call to Carina and his face flushed; had he really done that? Of course he had. He wished there was some way to recall a phone message that hadn't yet been played, but he had no idea whether Carina had heard it yet or not. Maybe she'd deleted it instantly, or maybe it was still sitting there, tormenting her the way every thought of her tormented him.

The bartender set the bottle of water on the bar and Finn signed for it, charging the five dollars to his room.

"Captain Finn!" Elise's voice rang out through the lobby and the sound of her sandals clicked against the floors as she walked over to the bar. "Hi, honey. How's tricks?"

Finn took a big gulp of water and screwed the cap back on the bottle. "Hey, Elise. Not too bad."

"You're looking pretty lonely for a married man," she said with a wink, stopping right in front of him and leaning an elbow on the bar. "Or are you two officially separated?"

Finn wanted to give her the kind of "Ha ha ha" that a middle schooler might give a teasing friend, but instead he smiled good-naturedly. "I think we've decided to go our separate ways. Except she'll be here with us to watch the regatta, I'd imagine."

"Oh, she's here." Elise turned her body back toward the center of the lobby and waved a hand at where Lucy stood, smiling and nodding while a very short bald man gestured wildly as he spoke to her. "Looks like she's been corralled by that old guy from Omaha. He's a talker, that one."

Finn nodded and held onto his water bottle tightly as he fought to keep the smile off his face. "Well, some people do love to talk," he said mildly.

"Listen, Finn. I need to tell you everything that's happened. You won't believe how well things are going, honey." Without asking, Elise took his arm and steered him toward the knot of people waiting to board the vans to watch the regatta. "Let's hang out together, shall we? My boyfriend is busy on his boat today," she said, looking like a teenage girl with a crush. "And I've already started making plans for his birthday next month."

Just then, Lucy glanced their way and lifted a hand in greeting. Finn nodded back at her. He leaned forward so that he was closer to Elise as she talked, intending to give her his full attention. It wasn't that he was transfixed by her love story, but more that he wanted to do something, *anything*, to keep his mind occupied and off his phone message to Carina.

"You two already have plans for next month?" he asked, pointing at the sliding glass doors as the rest of their crew started to move in that direction. Lucy led the way, walking backward and motioning with both hands like a tour guide as she gave instructions for the day.

"Well, I already have plans for the rest of our lives," Elise clarified, putting one manicured hand to her chest, "but he has yet to be informed about all of that." She said this like it was a minor detail to be ironed out, but her face was deadly serious.

"Wow. I admire your confidence."

"Confidence comes with life experience," Elise said, letting Finn help her into the van as they followed the short, bald man from the lobby and his wife, who refused to climb all the way to the back and instead took the front seats. Elise shot them a withering look. "And once you know who you are and where you belong, you'll have it. I promise."

Finn settled in next to Elise in the back seats, buckling his seat belt as she searched around for hers. "Here you go," he said, offering her the end of the belt that had been tucked between the seats.

"Thank you, honey. Now," Elise said, fastening her seatbelt with a click. "It's been a few days since we met, and I want to know more about this woman you left behind, the poor thing. I bet you broke her damn heart."

Finn watched out the window as the vans pulled out of the hotel's driveway and started to make their way toward their destination. The water was visible from Elise's side of the van and he stared at it, transfixed by the spot where the water met the sky.

"Oh, I don't know," he said, clearing his throat. "There's not much to tell."

"A gorgeous young man comes on a group trip all alone to a glamorous spot halfway around the world—do not lie to me, child, there is a *story* there." Elise reached for his water bottle, uncapped it, and took a swig like she'd just grabbed his martini off the bar and sipped it without being offered.

"Okay," Finn said, laughing a little. Elise hadn't stopped surprising him yet. "Not many people know this." He cleared his throat again and dropped his voice. Elise leaned closer. "Carina and I are...not the same age. In fact, she's closer to your age than mine."

"OH. MY. GOD." Elise swatted his arm forcefully with each word. "I knew it! You're one of those delicious men who looks like everything is right there on the surface, but you're like a deep, dark pond. Oooh, I *love* a mysterious man!"

Finn clasped his hands and looked down at them, nodding. "I guess," he said, feeling slightly uncomfortable. He never thought of himself as anything but a regular guy, but maybe there was something more there that he was too close to identify. "Anyway, Carina is fifty-one, and as you know, I'm about to turn thirty."

"Oh, honey," Elise said in a conspiratorial whisper. "This is *hot*—you do know that, right? A woman really comes into her own at that age, and she's finally able to give a man...well, everything. Her mind, her wisdom, her body." Elise paused, shaking her head. "If I'd known a man your age when I was fifty, that would have been a nice distraction to the loneliness and turmoil I was going through as a widow raising two children alone." Her eyes looked faraway as she imagined it.

Finn turned his head and looked her directly in the eye. "But it was more than just a distraction for either of us," he said, his voice sounding hoarse with emotion. "I loved her, Elise. I still love her."

Elise's brow furrowed and she searched his face. "Then what was the problem, doll? Is she married?"

"No, no," Finn said, shaking his head firmly. "Nothing like that. It's just, we live in a pretty small town, and Carina was—I mean, like over ten years ago—she was my teacher. In high school."

Elise stared at him, mouth slightly open. "Oh wow. Finn."

"But we just met up a couple of years ago at a retirement party and reconnected. It was nothing like what you're thinking. Nothing at all," he added hurriedly, taking his water bottle back from her so that he had something to hold onto. "I think I was a C student in her class, and when we started talking at the party she remembered me, but we had never had any personal discussions when I was a kid, so it was like meeting someone for the first time, essentially."

"Except that someone was a hot high school teacher who probably showed up in your dreams at least once or twice at sixteen, right?"

Finn's face went red. "Hey," he said, turning the hand that wasn't holding the water bottle toward the ceiling of the van as he gave a guilty shrug. "I never said I didn't think she was pretty, it just wasn't like *that*."

"I hear you," Elise said, putting a soft hand on his bare knee and patting it reassuringly. "And I'm not judging. Two people's happiness is something to celebrate, not denigrate." Her face was serious. "So why isn't she here with you? What went wrong?"

Finn peeled at the label of the water bottle like a nervous kid. It was hard to admit out loud that their differences had been too much for Carina but not for him. It made him feel like he should have found some fault with their age difference when he truly hadn't.

"I guess she thought I was too young." He shrugged. "Although what she said was basically that she was too old. She was worried I'd want kids or something. I don't know."

When he finally turned to look at Elise again, she was watching him. "I think her bigger concerns were probably that someday— sooner than she'd like—you might look at her and not see that beautiful, desirable, intelligent person you love, but that you'd instead see an aging woman. Someone whose health might be shifting, and whose body would undoubtedly change in ways you might not find as pleasing."

"That's pretty much what she said," Finn admitted. "But it's not true. I love *her*. I don't love her in spite of or even because of her age, I just simply love her."

Elise took his hand in hers and held it, but it felt soothing. Almost motherly. "She's a lucky woman," she said, looking out the window instead of at Finn. "A lucky woman indeed. And I hope she comes to her senses, Finn. There aren't as many opportunities in life for true love as you might think."

Finn watched her profile as she squinted out at the glare off the water. Instead of saying anything, he squeezed her hand lightly.

"So hey," Elise said, looking back at him with a bright smile. "Let me tell you about how I sent an email to Bradford's daughter this morning."

Finn blinked a few times in surprise. "You what?"

"I used my powers of persuasion on the front desk girl and got his emergency contact information."

"Okay, I'm listening." Finn felt oddly unburdened by having told Elise about his feelings for Carina. He'd been keeping them bottled up so tightly to honor her wishes for secrecy back home that he hadn't even realized how good it felt to just talk about her. He took a deep breath and focused on Elise's excited face. "You obtained his personal details in an unsavory fashion and then you emailed his daughter. I'm gonna need more."

"So," Elise said, keeping her voice low like they were being spied on by the CIA. "I want to plan a surprise birthday party for Bradford next month, and I'm going to fly in for it. Anyway, his daughter—"

"Wait, wait," Finn said, frowning and holding up a hand. "Elise, are you sure about this?"

Elise's smile faded. "Yes, of course I am. I'm great at planning parties and organizing. It's in my blood."

"No, not that part—just the idea of flying to his hometown and throwing him a surprise party after you've only known him a few days. Are you sure he's on the same page as you are in terms of the seriousness of this whole thing?"

"You mean the seriousness of our relationship?"

The van hit a bump in the road and both Elise and Finn reached out and grabbed the seat in front of them.

"Okay, like with that," Finn said slowly. "Are you sure he's even thinking of this as a relationship and not just a vacation fling?"

Elise blinked a few times. She looked taken aback. "Do you think I'm vacation fling material? I was hoping he saw me as something classier than that."

"Elise," Finn said, weighing his words like gold. "I think you are undoubtedly a woman of class, but sometimes men..." He squinted off into the distance as he gazed past her out the window. "Sometimes they don't think the same way that women do. Do you know what I'm saying?"

At this, Elise laughed heartily. "Do I know that men are dogs with one thing on their minds? Yes, doll, I do know that. But don't you think there are certain women who can tame a man more quickly than others? Haven't you ever known a woman who made you think of nothing but her? Who made you want her like you've never wanted anything else?" Her eyebrows raised as she waited for her questions to hit their mark, which of course they did. "Ahh, so you see what I mean?" she asked, nodding.

Finn looked appropriately chagrined. "Okay, I do get your point. There are those special women who capture your heart and your imagination, probably even for a dyed-in-the-wool bad boy, though I'm not saying your guy is bad. I'm sure he's amazing."

Elise beamed. "He's pretty special. I've gone out with a man or two since my Douglas passed, but none who I could really see a future with. I don't want to let this one get away."

Finn thought about this; it was hard to argue with not wanting to miss the opportunity to love someone when it felt right.

Elise shifted in her seat and looked out the window as the van pulled into a lot. "This must be the place. I can't wait to watch the regatta," she said, pulling a pair of oversized Jackie O type sunglasses from her purse. "I'm not sure if we'll see Bradford's yacht or not, but he's out there today."

They waited for the vans to unload, then Finn stood outside the sliding door and offered both hands to Elise to help her step down into the lot on her kitten heels. "You really dressed for the regatta," he said wryly, looking at her calf-length chiffon sundress and at the small purse looped over her elbow.

"I dressed to mingle and hobnob with the kind of people who own yachts and travel the world," she said haughtily, lifting her chin in the air slightly and extending a hand with her pinky up like she was holding a cup of tea.

Finn laughed. "Of course you did."

"Now let's go watch these puny little skiffs and cheer for my man, shall we?"

Finn held out an elbow gallantly, which Elise took. "That does seem to be the order of the day. And I heard that Lucy is having a lunch catered for us while we watch."

"Oooh!" Elise looked up at him like a little kid who'd just found out that there'd be cake. "I hope there's champagne and finger sandwiches!"

Finn shook his head. "I'm sure there will be. I don't think this is the kind of event for hot dogs and beer, is it?"

Elise wrinkled her nose. "Darling, no. Regattas are for old money, expensive booze, and new shoes." She stopped and looked down at her hot pink suede sandals with their little heel.

Finn stopped beside her and looked down at them. "I guess I didn't get the memo on that, because I just wore my old Birkenstocks."

Elise waved a hand and led them over to the collection of chairs Lucy had ordered for them so that they could watch from the beach. "Oh, you're just fine like that too. Did you know that the really, extravagantly, violently rich prefer to wear things that look like they shop at Target? I read that somewhere. They skip the labels and the fuss and just shlep around." She shrugged. "So really, you look richer than I do."

"Well, I can assure you that a fireman from a small town is pretty much the opposite of rich. But hey, if I look like Bill Gates here in my no-name t-shirt and khaki shorts, then so be it."

Just then, Lucy spotted them and waved. She pointed at two chairs on the sand.

Elise stopped in her tracks and looked down at her shoes. "Well, I did not plan for this. Thank god I got a pedicure before this trip." She kicked off the sandals and bent over to pick them up. "A gal's gotta be game, you know? And I'm nothing if not game." She winked at Finn.

"You know, I can see that about you, Elise. You are one heck of an adventurous lady."

Elise squeezed his arm and then let it go. She made a beeline for the chairs Lucy had pointed to, and Finn changed direction and headed for the table laden with snacks and drinks.

The yachts were visible in the distance, their giant sails caught on gusts of wind that made them look like giant, muscular men with their chests puffed up proudly. Elise was already deep in conversation with a woman from the tour group, so Finn picked up half a turkey sandwich on wheat and put it on a small plate with a slice of pineapple, a slice of watermelon, and a scoop of red potato salad with green peas and dill. The cooler at the end of the table held bottles of beer, tiny bottles of Prosecco, and ice cold cans of soda. Finn chose a Coke to start with, and then perched on a bench far from the rest of the guests.

As he took a bite of the sweet, tart pineapple, he watched the other guests from their group mingle and laugh together. Lucy was making the rounds, chatting with each person and making sure everyone felt comfortable. It was a job he didn't envy. People were tough; keeping them happy was even tougher.

Finn was halfway through his sandwich when his phone buzzed in his shorts pocket, and he set his plate next to the can of Coke on the bench and fished out the phone that was ringing against his thigh. As he did, his heart nearly stopped.

There on the screen was a face he knew almost as well as his own: it was Carina.

14

MARCH 20

ST. BARTS

"Finn?" Carina's voice filled his ear. It was like music; it felt familiar; it was home. "Where are you? Are you okay?"

Finn stood up and walked away from the bench, leaving his lunch behind as he walked closer to the water and farther from the other onlookers. For a moment, his words caught in his throat.

"I'm good. How are you?" Finn was aiming for casual, but it was hard to hold his composure, so he stared out into the distance, letting the bright sky dry his eyes.

"Well," Carina laughed. "You're going to think I'm crazy."

"I don't think that," he assured her, shaking his head although she couldn't see him.

Carina's laugh filled his ears again. "Hang on. You might." She paused. "I'm at your hotel."

Finn nearly dropped the phone. His skin went cold and clammy. "What? Are you kidding?"

"No," she said, sounding slightly less sure of herself. "I got your message and I don't want to say I panicked, but there was something in your voice, and I...I don't know. It was like everything was suddenly out of my hands. Before I knew what was happening, I'd bought myself a plane ticket and now, well, here I am."

Finn breathed in and out, watching the water ebb and flow as people shouted and cheered around him. In the distance, the yachts raced across the channel, their colorful sails breaking up the endless blue of the sky and the water.

"God...Carina. I need to get back there." Finn put a hand to his head and left it there as he quickly ran through the possibilities. "I'm at the regatta and I came with a bunch of people in a van. Uhhh, damn it. Okay, I'll find a way."

"Finn?" Carina said, her voice sounding happy again. "You're not mad I'm here?"

"What? No! Hell no. I just want to get to you as fast as I can."

"Stay where you are," she said, "I'll leave my bags with the bellhop and get an Uber from here to wherever you are."

"But I don't know where I am exactly," Finn said, still feeling like his brain wasn't putting the pieces of the puzzle together quickly enough.

Carina's voice was muffled for a moment as she conferred with someone on her end. "The concierge says he knows where you are and he'll help me get to you."

Finn's heart flipped wildly in his chest. "You are serious, right? This isn't some big joke?"

"Finn. I'll be there as soon as I can. Wait for me."

Carina ended the call and Finn stood there for a minute, looking at the scene around him. Everything was suddenly different: the sky was bluer; the boats on the water more thrilling; the sand under his feet more solid. Carina was here—she was coming to him.

Twenty minutes later, as he stood at the front of the parking lot that led to the beach area, a gray Mercedes pulled in and came to a stop. Finn had to keep himself from hopping from foot to foot like an anxious little kid (an image he never wanted of himself, given their age difference and the potential for him to actually *be* a kid in Carina's eyes).

The door to the car swung open and out stepped Carina, looking as beautiful as Finn remembered. He was frozen to the spot for a beat, watching as she said goodbye to the driver, who turned around and pulled back out of the lot.

In spite of other people parking and retrieving things from their cars, they were alone. The presence of anyone else didn't matter. A slight breeze lifted the light skirt that Carina wore and blew her blonde hair around. There were times when she argued with Finn, insisting that he see the crow's feet around her eyes or that he acknowledge the shiny streaks of silver that peppered her blonde highlights, but he would never acquiesce. Sure, they were there, but what Finn saw was real beauty: dancing blue eyes that shone with love and curiosity; the legs of a dancer; a smile that could stop traffic with teeth so well-cared for that it made him feel like he needed to do a better job taking care of himself—even in his twenties.

"Hey," Carina said, holding the purse that hung from one shoulder and shifting her weight nervously from one sandaled foot to the other. Rather than walking over to him, she kept her distance, standing about ten feet away. "You said in your message that weird things had happened." Her eyes locked on his and they held one another's gaze. "I know I said that you couldn't be, but are you still mine, Finn?"

"I'm still yours," he said without hesitation. The worried look in her eyes dissipated. "And I still want you to be mine."

Finally, Carina's gaze skimmed the parking lot. "Even with all of our differences?"

"Our differences never mattered to me," he said, not looking away from her. God, she was stunning. Regardless of her insistence that in ten, twenty, even—unfathomably—thirty years he might not feel the same, he knew what he felt in his heart, and that was pure, devoted love for this woman standing before him. "I like the things that make you who you are, and I'm not ashamed of the things that make me who I am."

Carina bit her lip and he watched as she processed everything, sifting through the facts, the feelings, the emotions, the consequences of their love. It took her less than five seconds.

"I missed you so much." Carina let go of her purse and closed the distance between them in just a few steps. She threw her arms around Finn and held him tightly. "I don't care what happened," she whispered in his ear as he slid his arms around her warm, familiar body, "I don't want to lose you again. Not for a second. Not because we don't like the same music. Not because our parents or anyone around us might disapprove. Not for anything."

Finn pulled her as close to his body as he possibly could without things getting too steamy for a beach parking lot at noon.

"I won't let you out of my arms again, Carina," he whispered into her hair as he drew in her scent, closing his eyes. "I promise."

She pulled back and looked at him, their faces just an inch apart. And then she leaned in and put her lips to his, gently at first and then more insistently, one foot lifting off the ground as they lost themselves in the kiss.

And, for once, neither of them cared who was watching.

FROM HER SPOT IN THE BACK OF THE VAN WITH NICK, LUCY WATCHED Finn and this marvelous creature who had appeared at the regatta as they clung to one another, touching at all times. They held hands, or had arms around each other, brushing their faces together for a quick kiss here and there. It was amazing: Finn had been transformed. Gone was the slightly wistful, vaguely distant man who'd joined them on the trip just days ago. Gone was the hungover, regretful guy she'd woken up married to on Bradford's yacht, and in his place was this glowing, smiling, laughing man who gazed adoringly at the older woman at his side.

He'd brought Carina around, introducing her to Lucy, Nick, and Elise, and then immediately taken her to a spot on the sand where they'd kicked off their shoes and sat together, fingers laced together and heads bowed toward one another as they'd ignored the regatta and focused entirely on each other.

"This is crazy," Nick said in a low voice, leaning over so that his shoulder touched Lucy's. "Finn's got a girl who's old enough to be his mom? And she flew here on a whim to join him?"

Lucy gave him a look to show that it was all a mystery to her. "I guess so. Maybe he told her that we got married and she freaked out and hopped on the next flight."

Nick laughed softly. "I can honestly see where that might be the case. A guy you think you're done with marries another woman impulsively and suddenly he seems like a catch again."

Lucy's eyes narrowed as she watched Carina lay her blonde head on Finn's shoulder. "I don't think that's it," she said. "I feel like it's much deeper than that. Being a woman is hard, and being an older woman with a younger—much younger—man is even harder."

"You speak from experience?" Nick looked at her curiously, holding onto the headrest in front of him as they bumped their way over an unpaved lane on the way back to the hotel.

"Oh definitely," she said, her voice laced with sarcasm. "No, not really. I think I once dated a guy who was like nine months younger than me and it felt like I was robbing the cradle. It's not for me. But more power to them; they look over the moon, don't they?"

Nick assessed them. "Yeah...to be honest, they do."

The tired, sun-burnished, wind-swept crew straggled back into the bright, shiny lobby. Sunlight from outside bathed the marble floors and white accessories in a golden light that invited people to sink wearily into the couches and fan themselves as they watched the sun making its afternoon descent over the water. Elise flagged down a speed-walking waiter with an empty tray and ordered a drink, taking off her sunhat and laying it next to her on the couch with her sunglasses.

Lucy stopped in her tracks as she spotted Alvin and a knot of hotel staff behind the counter, huddled and looking serious. There was a police officer dressed in discreet but official attire, standing near them with a cell phone pressed to his ear. Lucy glanced over at Nick, who had also clocked the situation. They gave each other questioning looks.

"Should I try to see what's going on?" Lucy asked. "I don't want to be nosy, but we are taking up a good chunk of the hotel, so if something's going on that our group needs to know about then I should probably get the details."

Nick watched the hotel staff confer with the cop, who had ended his phone call. They all looked extremely serious. "I'm not sure," he said. He folded his arms across his chest and surveyed the lobby. All of the Holiday Adventure Clubbers were deep in conversation, discussing the gorgeous afternoon, the allure of the pool, their plans for dinner, or whether it was too early for a drink, which, for Elise, who was taking a margarita from the hands of the busy waiter, it clearly was not. "Maybe?"

Without thinking twice, Lucy walked over to the desk. She'd been in many situations in her former life where she'd had to deal with police officers delivering bad (sometimes extremely tragic) news, and there wasn't much that could throw her.

"He's at the Hôpital de Bruyn," the police officer was saying, looking at his phone screen as he relayed some information. "And currently in critical condition."

Alvin nodded, keeping a serious face as the woman next to him covered her mouth, eyes wide in horror. "I just helped him this morning," she said, her French accent soft and lilting.

"We can get you the contact information," Alvin said, clearing his throat and stepping up to the computer. He tapped at the keys, face stoic as he wrote down some information on a notepad and handed it over to the police officer.

"Thank you." The officer gave a curt, single nod, took the piece of paper, and walked out to the pool area, stopping by the palm trees where Lucy had had her phone conversation with her mother on St. Patrick's Day.

"Hi, Alvin," Lucy said gently, placing both palms on the counter to show that she was calm and not there to ask him for anything. Everyone behind the desk looked completely shell-shocked, and other than Alvin, they were whispering frantically to one another in French. "I hope everything is okay," she started. "Is there anything we need to know as a group to make things smoother here? Do you need us to get out of here for a while and have dinner off-site or anything?"

Alvin took a deep breath, held it in his chest, and when he released it, he gave a professional, perfunctory smile. "Everything is fine, Miss Landish," he said evenly. As soon as the words were out of his mouth, his face fell. "Actually, they are not fine."

Lucy nodded, waiting.

"Two of the boats collided at the regatta, and one of our guests is in critical condition. It happened in the final minutes of the race, and the police are not sure yet which boat was at fault."

A cold rush of chills sparkled up and down Lucy's spine and both arms. She actually gave an involuntary shiver. "Oh god," she said. "Was it..."

Alvin gave a serious nod. "Yes, it was the man your friend has been spending time with," he said, looking across the lobby to where Elise was standing, holding her margarita gingerly as she tried to walk carefully across the marble floor in her kitten heels. "Bradford Melton."

Lucy closed her eyes and held them that way for a long moment. "It was him. Okay." She nodded a few times and opened her eyes. "I guess I should let Elise know, since, as you said, she's been spending time with him." Lucy broached the topic from that angle, knowing that spreading information about an accident and a man in the hospital to other guests might be a faux pas, given that Bradford's family didn't even know yet. She waited for Alvin's confirmation.

"Yes, Miss Landish. You should probably tell her." He leaned across the desk so that they were able to speak in a near whisper. "I'm not sure if her things are in his room, but his family will be arriving and she might want to retrieve her belongings."

Lucy patted the counter delicately with both hands, which were still flat on the marble. "Yes," she said, her mind spinning. "You're so right. I'll go and speak with her now. Thank you, Alvin," she said, giving him a smile to let him know that she was going to be discreet.

Elise had slipped into the computer room off the side of the lobby, and although there was a sign with a tropical looking drink that had a giant X over it and the words "No Food or Beverages Near Computers," she was sitting on a chair, back straight, drink held aloft in one hand as she typed in her password to her email account with one manicured finger.

"Oh, hi, doll," she said, catching sight of Lucy. She spun in the chair and took a sip of her drink. "I'm just working on a little project here." She dropped her voice like she was about to deliver a state secret. "I emailed Bradford's daughter to plan a surprise party for his birthday. I think he's gonna love it."

"Listen, Elise," Lucy said, pulling one of the other rolling chairs away from an empty computer and sitting down. She scooted closer to Elise so that their knees were almost touching. "I have some news and it might be upsetting. Actually, it will be upsetting. You might want to set your drink down." She motioned to the margarita and then glanced at the desk.

Elise set the frosty glass next to the keyboard, her face expectant. "Oh, honey. What's up? You gotta tell me. Don't keep an old gal on the edge like this."

Lucy took a breath. "The police were just here, and apparently there was an accident at the regatta. In the last couple of minutes, right after we left, two yachts collided and one of them was Bradford's. He's in the hospital." She reached out and took both of Elise's hands in hers. "I'm so sorry."

The computer screen changed over Elise's shoulder, and her inbox popped up. Lucy glanced at it.

"I need to go to the hospital," Elise said, standing up slowly. Her legs wobbled slightly under her and her face looked ashen. "I just met him, but I have a good feeling about Bradford. I think he's the one, Lucy. I really do. I have to be there in case he needs me. I can't lose him."

Lucy nodded. She had no idea what the right move was here, given the brevity of Elise and Bradford's relationship, but it wasn't really her call to make. "I can help you get an Uber. Are you ready to head over?"

Elise nodded. She walked away from her nearly full drink and left her email open on the screen. Lucy would come back and deal with all of that in a minute.

In short order, Lucy had Elise tucked into the back of a car out front, she'd taken Bradford's room key from her and promised to get the makeup bag and clothes that Elise had left strewn around his room, and then she was left standing beneath the stone portico to the hotel, listening to the artificial waterfall as it trickled down the rocks.

What a day. A surprise arrival (Did she have room for one more person in the official group? Carina had promised she'd be no trouble, and of course there was room—no problem). And now a tragic accident with an undecided outcome. Lucy stood still for a moment, letting it all sink in. She suddenly remembered the computer and the margarita and Elise's belongings in Bradford's room, and she snapped out of her thoughts and went inside to deal with the wreckage of this emergency.

Standing in front of the computer, Lucy picked up the melting margarita. There, on the screen, was Elise's email inbox, with a new message in bold: it was from Michelle Melton, and the subject was *Re: Allow me to introduce myself...*

The temptation to read it and find out what sort of mess Elise was getting herself into was strong, but Lucy batted it away immediately. After all, Elise was not her mother and therefore not her problem. She had her own maternal baggage to deal with, and she didn't need to take on anyone else's mom, even on a trip. Before she could give it more thought, she logged out of the account, turned off the computer screen, and walked the margarita back to the bar where she deposited it on the counter. It was time to pick up Elise's stuff and drop it off with Alvin so that he could have it delivered directly to the room of its rightful owner.

She promised herself in the elevator that she'd simply walk in, grab the things she needed to grab, and get out of the room. The forensic pathologist in her wanted to eyeball the details, to take it all in and start piecing together a puzzle, but Lucy had to remind herself that she wasn't a detective, that figuring out what had befallen a human body wasn't at all the same as deciphering a relationship or a living person's motives. And most of all, it wasn't her business.

As she gathered Elise's items, her phone buzzed: it was Nick.

"Hey, you okay?" he asked without preamble.

"I'm good. Where are you?" Lucy put the phone on speaker and set it on a table as she shoved Elise's nightgown and make up into a laundry bag she'd found in the closet.

"Hanging out at the pool, waiting to see how I can help."

"You know what would really help? If you could order me a vodka tonic with lime? I'll be right down." Lucy cinched the drawstring of the laundry bag and took one last look around.

"Your wish is my command, boss. See you in a few."

CARINA AND FINN WERE IN THE POOL WHEN LUCY ARRIVED, HAVING dropped the bag of Elise's stuff off at the counter to a worried-looking Alvin. Carina had her arms around Finn's neck and they were floating together, smiling into each other's eyes like they'd just discovered that the sun rose and set in one another's irises.

"So," Lucy said, flopping onto the chair next to Nick's as she nodded at the lovebirds in the pool. "Looks like Finn's on his way to a pretty solid vacation now."

Nick handed her a tumbler with clear liquid on ice and a wedge of lime. "Yeah, I think he's gotten over your divorce in record time."

"Much like my first husband," Lucy said, raising her glass in the air before taking a sip.

"Ouch." Nick winced and then smiled at her, watching her face as she took another drink and started to relax.

"Waking up next to a stranger and being married—even fake married—will be a story I laugh at in the future, I'm sure. At the moment it still feels fairly ridiculous. Do you think he's told Carina?"

They looked at the couple in the pool as they laughed and Finn pulled her closer.

"Well," Nick said, "maybe? She is an older woman with a lot more life experience than he has, so it's possible she can take a plot twist like that in stride. On the other hand, she hightailed it down here, so maybe he called and told her and she freaked out. Women are something of a mystery to me." He shrugged lightly and took a sip of the beer that he'd been holding in one hand.

"Hey, did I tell you that Elise emailed Bradford's adult daughter to start planning a surprise birthday party for him next month? She wants to fly in for it and arrange the whole thing."

Nick turned his head slowly and made an incredulous face. "No, she did not. Does her guy know about this?"

"Well, given that it's a surprise party, I'd say no."

"Terrible idea." Nick sipped his beer again and shook his head. "Bad move."

A mellow jazz track was playing from the speakers in the bar, and the sounds drifted out to the patio area as two waiters circled, taking drink orders from everyone, even the people in the pool.

"You think?" Lucy frowned. "I thought it was kind of forward, but still sweet."

"I think it's kind of crazy with a side helping of crazy. They just met. He's gonna hate it."

"Epperson, for a writer you seem to have very little imagination," Lucy quipped. "I think it's romantic."

"I think it's invasive. What if he's married?"

Lucy's head snapped around to look at him. "What? No way. He's been carrying on with Elise for days now, letting her sleep in his room and charge things to his tab. What kind of married man would act that way?"

Nick wisely put his beer bottle to his lips and gazed out at the water without saying a word.

"Oh god," Lucy said, understanding washing over her. "My own husband carried on this way. I mean, not with trips to tropical islands and yachts and stuff, but on a smaller scale. He was taking a female coworker to dinner and telling me it was so expensive because it was his turn to buy for his buddy Adam. He even went on a 'work trip' to Philly and shared a room with this woman. Damn. I'm such an idiot."

Nick put a hand on her knee. "No you're not. And Elise isn't either. You're hopeful and trusting and you believe in love. Those are all good qualities."

Lucy chewed on her lower lip as she watched Finn swim over to the side of the pool to sign for two glasses of champagne that the waiter was delivering on a tray.

"You're right. I just hope for Elise's sake that this guy is legit. She came on this trip looking to find someone, so of course I want that for her. But I hope she doesn't fall for some phony just because he's got money."

"She seems like a fairly put together lady," Nick said in a noncommittal tone. In fact, neither of them knew Elise well enough to say whether or not that was true, but Lucy certainly hoped it was. "Hey," Nick said, shifting gears. "Everyone is on their own tonight for dinner, right?"

Lucy nodded, sipping her vodka tonic.

"Can I take you out? I know we're waiting to hear about the situation at the hospital, but Elise has your number, and we both need to eat, so..." He drained his beer and set the empty bottle on the little side table. "What do you say?"

"Can we have pizza?"

Nick looked at her with a wry smile. "The lady comes to a French island but wants pizza. Huh."

"Hey, sometimes you just want what you want."

"Indeed you do," Nick agreed. "Pizza it is."

15

MARCH 20

ST. BARTS

Without bothering to change out of their regatta clothes, Nick and Lucy had set out to find a place that served pizza. They'd found a place on a busy street, tucked in between an expensive jewelry store and a doctor's office, and to their surprise, the hostess had led them through the restaurant and out to a back patio made of terra cotta bricks. Strings of lights criss-crossed the open seating area, and tables for two dotted the space, filled with couples leaning close to one another over flickering candles as they shared bottles of wine and plates of pasta.

"Wow, this is gorgeous," Lucy said, feeling breathless as she took in the view of the water from over the railing of the patio. She'd had no idea that the street itself backed up to a bluff with a view of the marina and the open waters beyond. "And I'm starving." Nick pulled out her chair for her and waited for Lucy to get situated. "I was so busy checking on everyone else and meeting Finn's girlfriend at the regatta that I forgot to eat anything from the buffet spread that I spent so much time planning."

"Let's remedy that right away." Nick signaled a waiter so they could order a bottle of wine and an appetizer.

"Any further word on Honey or the robbery back home?" Nick asked, leaning back in his chair after putting in their drink order.

"Oh god," Lucy groaned. "With everything else going on I completely forgot about that." She put both hands to the sides of her face and looked pained. "How could I have forgotten?"

"When you're in another country, it's forgiven. Sometimes you get caught up in what's going on in front of your face, you know?"

"Yeah, but I'm generally not an 'out of sight, out of mind' kind of person. Not at all."

Nick was holding his fork in one hand, using the handle of it to gently trace a pattern along the tabletop as he listened. "So, when you were in Venice, did you think about me, or did you forget about the old Carrier Pigeon and your buddy Nick because we weren't right there?"

Lucy's face flushed; she *had* thought of him. "I called you, didn't I? And I texted on Valentine's Day." Lucy leaned forward in her seat, warming to the subject. "In fact, I'm pretty sure I was the one who reached out first both times, wasn't I? So maybe I'm not the one suffering from 'out of sight, out of mind-itis.'"

Nick laughed. "Did you just coin a new term? Identify a new medical diagnosis?" He set his fork on his napkin and folded his hands on his lap casually.

"Maybe I did." Lucy gave her long, loose hair a toss, flipping it over her shoulders as she considered him. "But then, you did travel to another country with me, so I guess that counts for something."

"Oh, it does?" Nick laughed again. "Like maybe I'm making progress with my disease?"

"I feel like progress is being made," Lucy said with a smile, looking up at their server as he appeared with two glasses and a bottle of red wine. The waiter uncorked the bottle, poured each of them a glass, and waited as they took their first sips. "Delicious," Lucy said to him as he bowed slightly and walked away.

They were quiet for a long minute as they sipped wine and watched the people around them. Beyond the railing was an evening sky of orange and pink that faded into the horizon as the sun sank towards the water. It was easy to push everything aside in that moment, to forget home, robberies, boat accidents, drunken weddings, and surprise girlfriends showing up on the island. There was nothing in that moment except their glasses of smooth, rich wine, the watercolor skies, and each other.

Lucy smiled shyly at Nick.

"Hey," he said, setting his wine glass down. "This might seem like a bizarre thing to say, but I really enjoy your company."

Lucy threw back her head and laughed. "Oh yes, it is completely bizarre for a man to enjoy my company. Thank you for clarifying that."

"No," Nick said, looking down at the table. "What I meant to say is that it's been a long time since I've enjoyed anyone's company." He lowered his voice but lifted his eyes to meet Lucy's gaze. "For a long time after I lost Daisy, I didn't enjoy anything. I couldn't bring myself to leave the house much, so I read a lot, I wrote a lot—three of my best-selling books were written in the midst of crushing grief—and I definitely didn't think about love. I wasn't even sure I was capable of it anymore."

Lucy's heart rate picked up at the mention of love. She knew this feeling: the inability to put past hurts behind her and look ahead. There were times she'd even questioned herself about whether she'd agreed to date Charlie when she'd arrived on Amelia Island simply because he was an obvious dead-end, thus offering her a self-fulfilling prophecy of aloneness and misery. Sometimes after a big upheaval and a broken heart, what you really needed was to be allowed to carry around a chip on your shoulder that would keep everyone away—at least for a while.

"I get that," she said to Nick, holding onto the stem of her wine-glass and moving it around slowly on the table.

"But you're easy to be with, Lucy. Whenever you walk through the front door of my shop, my mood lightens. Your face makes me happy."

Again, Lucy felt the flush of pleasure that came with his words. "I feel the same way when I see you."

The waiter materialized then with their appetizer and set it down quietly between them on the table. Neither reached for it.

"I'm really glad I came along to St. Barts, Lucy." Nick held her gaze. "I mean, I felt like I might have missed my chance when I got sick that evening and you ran off and married that younger guy, but now that I know it was only a drunken fling, I feel much better." He winked at her and picked up a piece of the fried calamari on the plate in front of him.

"Yes, that was a close call," Lucy said, rolling her eyes. "I almost sailed off into the sunset with a fireman ten years my junior."

Nick shrugged. "Hey, no judgment. If a lady can still pull the younger men, then she's got it going on, you know?"

Lucy picked up a piece of calamari and dipped it in the creamy lemon-basil sauce that had come in a ramekin with their appetizer. "Oooh, this is good," she said, closing her eyes as she chewed. "Try the sauce."

Nick grabbed another bite and dipped it in the sauce. "You're right: this is amazing. We've only been here a few days and I already feel like I've put on twenty pounds."

"You haven't," Lucy said, taking a sip of her wine so that she wouldn't gorge on calamari and ruin her dinner. "But I can already see that we'll get home feeling like we need to detox. I never drink this much—I don't do cocktails on weeknights, and I definitely never drink enough to wake up married."

Nick laughed appreciatively. "That's probably for the best. And hey, speaking of gorgeous women who can snag younger men, what do we really think of Finn and his lady? Are they a love match?"

Lucy gave in and dragged another piece of calamari through the lemon-basil sauce before popping it in her mouth. She smiled gleefully. "She was his high school English teacher."

Nick gave a low whistle. "Damnnnnn," he said, shaking his head. "Young men everywhere just felt a glimmer of hope at that story."

Lucy reached across the table and swatted Nick's bare forearm. "Nick, stop! He told me that there was nothing whatsoever between them until they bumped into one another a couple of years ago and started talking. And apparently she's very hesitant to make their relationship public."

"What's the age difference?"

"Uhhh, I think Finn said he was about to turn thirty, and I'd say she's around fifty."

Nick nodded as he thought about it. "That sounds pretty decent, to be perfectly honest."

"You could be with a woman twenty years older than you?"

"Sure. I could do it. Some guys couldn't, but I've gotta say, there are a lot of indecisive, immature women out there. When a man has his head screwed on straight, sometimes he doesn't want to play around with a girl when he could find himself a woman."

Lucy put her wine glass to her lips and drank, watching Nick's face. She set her glass on the table. "And you've dated both?"

Nick tilted his head to one side, letting his mouth curve into a smile. "I have. I once dated a girl fifteen years younger than me and that was not the move—not for me anyway. And I dated a woman twelve years older than me, which worked out infinitely better. Ultimately, it didn't work out on a permanent level, but we had *a lot* of fun."

Lucy held up a hand. "Okay, okay. I get it. No details, please." She was starting to feel the buzz of wine in her head on top of the vodka tonic she'd had by the pool that afternoon.

Nick's smile grew wider. "I'm not trying to make you jealous, Dr. Landish, I'm just saying we got each other. And the fact that she knew who she was and what she wanted was really attractive to me."

"And now? Any preferences?" Lucy ventured, swallowing. She resisted another sip of wine, opting instead to stay as clear-headed as possible while they were on this topic.

"I can't say I have strong preferences about specifics," Nick said honestly. Their waiter passed by with a delicious looking pizza for the table behind them, and they both watched as he set it down. "I've never been one who insists on dating only blondes or only short and curvy girls."

"Both of those demands would take me out of the running," Lucy said out loud before she could stop herself. "I'm tall, kind of twiggy, and not a blonde." She ticked each item off on her fingers.

Nick looked at the candle on their table before returning his gaze to Lucy's face. "Did you want to be in the running?"

Lucy's heart pounded against her ribcage like a fist beating against a locked door, and Nick's eyes burned hotly as he waited to hear what she'd say. But before she could answer, their waiter walked up to the table with the ham, arugula, and fig pizza they'd ordered to share. They broke eye contact and leaned back in their seats like two fighters returning to their respective corners of the ring.

"Saved by the bell," Nick said, watching as the waiter slid a piece of pizza onto a plate and set it in front of Lucy, then did the same for him. "Thank you," he said to the waiter.

Once they were alone again, Lucy picked up her knife and fork. "This looks incredible," she said, cutting into her slice of pizza and taking the first bite. She'd wanted more of the conversation they'd finally started, but the waiter showing up with the pizza had shifted the mood, and now what she wanted was to save it for a time when they were truly alone, and not seated back-to-back with other people who were drinking and eating pizza by candlelight.

She got her wish after dinner as they strolled down the street together, stopping to look in the windows of all the shops.

"What do you think of going down to the water?" Nick asked, standing behind Lucy's left shoulder as she stared into the window of a store filled with silk scarves dyed to look like undulating blue waves and golden-hued sunsets over the sand. "I think there's a walkway just down the street and we could go down and hang out on the beach if you want."

Lucy turned around slowly so that they were facing each other. "I think that sounds nice," she said, reaching out and slipping her hand into his. His eyebrows lifted ever so slightly at the feeling of her fingers laced through his. "I love the beach at night."

Together, with the moonlight casting a warm glow across the sand and the water, they walked down a set of wooden stairs that led to the beach. There were other people scattered around, some walking, some sitting on blankets, but Lucy and Nick walked directly to the surf and took off their shoes, picking them up and holding them in their outside hands so that they could wind their fingers together again and hold hands as they walked. It was the purest, sweetest feeling Lucy had felt in a long time, and she smiled up at him as they strolled, feeling the cold, wet sand against the soles of her bare feet.

"So," Nick said, swinging the hand that held his shoes as he returned Lucy's look. "This has been a great trip. Watching everyone enjoy the island and seeing you in action as you lead the whole event is impressive."

"It's actually pretty easy once we're here," Lucy admitted. "Except for the unforeseen disasters, of course."

"Sure. But everything must be okay at the hospital, or I'm guessing we'd have heard. Maybe they already released Elise's guy with just some bandages and Advil."

"I hope so."

They stopped talking and walked for a couple of minutes in easy, companionable silence. Once they were a good distance from the last people they'd passed on the sand, Nick stopped walking but held Lucy's hand in his.

"Hey," he said, dropping his shoes. Lucy dropped hers and took his other hand so that they were facing one another with just inches between them. "You're something else, you know that?" Nick's voice was soft, but his words had meaning and insistence behind them. "I've been thankful for your friendship and for all the joy you bring into my life since the day I met you."

Lucy smiled, as a blush crept across her cheeks. She willed herself not to look away. "Same," she said, squeezing both of his hands. "I know that if I walk over to The Carrier Pigeon at any point during my day, I'm going to laugh at least five times. Not to mention that I get to see that handsome coworker of yours," she said, referring to Hemingway.

"He really is the one everyone comes to see," Nick said, making a self-deprecating face in the moonlight. His eyes sparkled beneath a fringe of lashes, and Lucy looked up at him, taking a step closer.

"Not me," she said gently, standing on her tiptoes and tilting her chin up so that her face was closer to his.

"Oh?" Nick tugged both of her hands lightly as he moved even closer. The heat from both of their bodies mingled as he slowly lowered his mouth toward hers. "You come there just to use my fax machine, don't you?" he said, his eyes still locked on hers.

Lucy couldn't help it: she giggled. "Stop," she said, pressing her chest against his as she let go of his hands and reached up to wrap both arms around his strong neck. "Stop teasing and just kiss me."

The waves lapped onto the shore, threatening the shoes they'd abandoned in the sand as Nick put his warm lips against Lucy's, kissing her softly at first, then with an urgency that could not be ignored.

Lucy pressed her body against the length of his and kissed him back with a fever she hadn't felt in years. This was Nick, her next door work neighbor. Nick, who joked and made her laugh everyday. Nick, who wrote murder mysteries and read every book under the sun. Nick, who'd lost a daughter and known his own heartbreak.

This was Nick, making her wild with desire. This was Nick, making her forget everything but the moon on the waves, the sand between her toes, his lips on hers. Lucy gave into it completely and kissed him the way she'd wanted to for a long time, and she didn't worry once about what it would mean tomorrow, or when they got back home.

Nothing mattered but that moment.

16

MARCH 21
ST. BARTS

A loud, insistent chirping woke Lucy. She'd never bothered to pull the curtains closed the night before, and now the morning filled the room completely.

The sound she'd at first thought was a bird on her balcony was actually her phone, and as Lucy rubbed her eyes and sat up, she reached for the nightstand and glanced down at her body—she was naked. She snatched the phone and flicked off the ringer, then turned her head slowly toward the other side of the bed, blinking a few times to clear her vision as she realized that Nick was there beside her.

Oh my god oh my god oh my god, Lucy chanted in her head, pulling the sheet up to cover her breasts. Nick didn't budge. He had a pillow over his face, but she knew without a doubt what had happened, and that he was probably grinning in his sleep. *So, okay, that happened,* she thought, running a hand through her hair as her phone buzzed in her other hand. With annoyance, she glanced at the screen and saw that she'd missed seven calls and eighteen texts.

As gently as possible, Lucy slipped her legs out from under the covers and stood up, feeling the warm sun against her naked body. It felt good, standing there, stretching as she watched Nick sleep. After all this time, it felt right. She tiptoed to the bathroom, phone still in hand. With the door closed, she turned on the shower and unlocked her phone screen to see what was going on.

They were all messages from Elise. *Lucy, can you come to the hospital? I need someone here—are you awake?* She skimmed the rest of the texts then glanced at the calls: again, all from Elise.

Lucy put her phone on the counter and stepped into the steaming shower. She had no idea what was going on at the hospital, but the rest of the Holiday Adventure Club would have to get by without her that morning as they took part in the parasailing and fishing excursions she'd lined up for them.

Within twenty minutes, she'd twisted her wet hair into a braid, and put on the minimum amount of makeup that she could get away with. As she stood at the dresser digging around for a pair of underwear, Nick propped himself up on one elbow, admiring her silhouette as she clutched a white towel around her body.

"Good morning," he said. Lucy spun around and saw the look on his face.

"Hey yourself." She smiled back.

"I think you left a dress over there." Nick pointed at a chair in the corner of the room where they'd both discarded everything they'd been wearing the night before.

"Yeah," Lucy said, nodding as she shut the drawer. She slipped a pair of panties on under the towel. "We definitely left a trail." She glanced around at the shoes, Nick's shirt and shorts, and her purse, which was open and spilling tubes of lipstick and coins onto the tile floor next to the balcony door. As the pennies and nickels glinted in the morning light, the memory of change tinkling across the tile when she'd dropped her purse the night before and of their laughter when Nick had told her to leave it all came rushing back. "So," she said, keeping the towel around her body as she walked over to the closet to find a new dress.

"So," Nick said, sitting up in bed. There, on his chest, was the daisy tattoo she'd seen during their FaceTime call when she'd been in Venice. The night before, as moonlight had streamed through the open windows, she'd traced the petals of the flower with her fingertips, realization dawning for the first time: the tattoo was for his daughter, Daisy. She hadn't known that the first time she'd seen it.

"How are you feeling?" Lucy slid a dress over her body, letting the towel fall to the floor as the fabric of the dress slipped down over her skin. She cinched the drawstring of the bust, glancing down to make sure that it really looked okay without a bra.

"In general, or about last night?"

Lucy kept her face toward the closet. "Either, I guess."

"I'm feeling pretty fantastic this morning," he said, making a loud sound as he stretched his arms overhead and got to his feet. Lucy turned to look at him and for the first time she was able to fully admire him. All of him. "And I'm also feeling pretty fantastic about last night. Where are we off to, Dr. Landish? Breakfast?"

"Actually," Lucy said, bending over to dig a pair of sandals out of the shoe bag she kept at the bottom of the closet. "Something urgent is going on at the hospital and Elise has been calling and texting me frantically, asking me to come over there."

Nick frowned and grabbed the pair of shorts he'd discarded the night before, pulling them on without underwear. His hair was mussed and he looked tired but happy.

"If you let me run back to my room to shower and change, I can come with you," he offered, reaching for his t-shirt to cover up his lean, muscled torso (which was a shame, in Lucy's opinion, because he looked so good straight out of bed.)

"No, you go ahead and take your time getting ready. It's possible she just wants some moral support and then I can bring her back to the hotel to relax since it seems like she's been there all night. If anything comes up, I'll call you. Otherwise I'll be back here ASAP and we can carry on with our day."

"Okay, boss," Nick said, pulling his shirt over his head and then giving her a casual, boyish salute. "Holler if you need me."

There was an awkward moment where Lucy wasn't sure if she should go to him, or if he was going to come over to her, and they stood there, both on the verge of making some uncertain move.

Finally, Nick laughed and opened his arms. "Come here," he said in a way that sounded both gruff and tender. Lucy went to him.

It was quick, but Nick pulled her to him and wrapped her in his arms, filling her with warmth as he brushed his lips over the top of her head. "I'm right here if you need me," he promised, letting go of her.

"I'll be quick." Lucy grabbed her purse and scooped up the coins and lipsticks that had escaped in the throes of their passion the night before, feeling somewhat sheepish as she did.

But there wasn't time for that, she realized, looking at her phone as it buzzed again with a message from Elise. With a quick wave at Nick over her shoulder, she headed down to the lobby to find a ride to the hospital.

"LUCY! LUCY!" ELISE STOOD UP FROM THE PLASTIC CHAIR SHE WAS occupying in a common area of the hospital's lobby. She looked tired and unsteady on her feet. "Thank god." The older woman walked over to Lucy, hands outstretched. Lucy took them in her own.

"What's going on? I'm sorry I missed all your calls, but I'm here now."

Elise sighed deeply, looking like she might cry. "Bradford is still in critical condition."

"What?" Lucy had imagined this yacht accident to be nothing more than one boat bumping another. She'd assumed that Bradford had maybe sprained an elbow or busted his lip. In truth, she knew from experience that things could have been much worse than that, but this was a vacation! A fun trip! Nothing bad was supposed to happen on a vacation. "Do you have any details?"

Elise sank down into the nearest chair like she could hardly keep herself upright. She hung onto one of Lucy's hands, effectively pulling her down into the chair next to hers. "He broke three ribs and punctured a lung, and there's talk of a concussion. But no one will tell me anything, mind you, given that I'm not his wife or any sort of blood relation, but I've been wandering past the nurse's desk all night, picking up bits and pieces of information as I go."

Lucy frowned. Bradford wasn't elderly, but he also wasn't a young buck, and punctured lungs and concussions could quickly progress to something more serious.

"Michelle is on her way," Elise added, opening her purse and searching for a Kleenex. "The night nurse and I bonded and she told me they'd contacted his next of kin, which is his daughter, of course."

The hospital lobby was bright with morning sunlight. The tall windows gleamed as palm trees swayed just outside, filtering the light as it spilled across the navy blue chairs and the carpet that was made of swirls of varying shades of blue. The whole effect was a calming one, though Lucy could imagine that most of the people who ended up waiting here felt anything but calm.

Just then, a tall, poised woman breezed through the automatic doors and into the lobby pulling a small rolling suitcase behind her. She stopped and looked from left to right, then pushed forward like she was totally accustomed to entering foreign situations and figuring things out on the fly.

Lucy watched her as she took long strides toward a desk against the wall that was occupied by a lone attendant in a white sweater and reading glasses. The woman with the suitcase stopped, tapped a finger against the desk, and asked a question. It was just a hunch, but Lucy felt like this might be Michelle.

"Hey," she said, squeezing Elise's hand. Elise startled and drew in a sharp breath. She looked like Lucy had woken her from a quick nap.

"I'm so glad you're here," Elise said, looking more vulnerable than Lucy would have imagined. Since the first day of the trip, when Elise had taken the microphone in the lobby of the hotel and given an impromptu performance, she'd come across as a strong, forthright presence without any inhibitions. Now she looked like a lost, confused woman who needed reassurance and guidance.

"I'm glad I'm here too," Lucy said, standing up and facing Elise, who was forced to look up at her. "Mostly because I know how to navigate this sort of thing. Let's head back to the nurse's station and I'll see if we can get any more information," she said, pulling Elise gently to her feet. Without asking, Lucy tucked the older woman's arm through hers and guided her like she might have done with her own mother, had she ever been able to get her mom to leave the house.

Sure enough, Lucy had been right: as they approached the counter where three nurses in scrubs were stationed behind two giant computer monitors and a bank of phones, the woman from the lobby was leaning against the handle of her suitcase, taking deep, fortifying breaths as she blinked at the whiteboard on the wall that was covered with the names of the nurses and their on-duty/off-duty status. Apparently Lisa, Corinne, and Edgar were on duty that morning, Lucy noted.

"Michelle Melton," the woman was saying as they approached. "I got a call that Bradford Melton had been in an accident and that it was serious, and I got on the first flight. I need to see him now," she said, making it a demand rather than a request.

Next to Lucy, Elise pulled herself up straighter and she smoothed the front of her wrinkled blouse.

"Do I look a mess, Lucy?" she whispered. "I know this isn't the time to care, but first impressions matter."

"You look great," Lucy assured her, watching Michelle Melton as she leaned across the desk and tried to see what the nurse was typing on the computer screen.

"Michelle?" Elise asked, stepping forward without Lucy as she cleared her throat. Michelle turned around brusquely, surprise written on her face. She was stunning, with perfectly arched eyebrows, nearly black hair, and pale, creamy skin. Her eyes were clear pools of blue. She looked like Snow White. "Hi, honey."

Michelle looked Elise up and down, her frown deepening. "Hello," she said tentatively.

"I'm Elise Rittenhour, your dad's girlfriend," Elise said, holding out a hand. "I emailed you the other day about the surprise party—
"

"I responded to your email," Michelle said, still watching Elise with narrowed eyes, still assessing her. "And my father is dead."

Elise blinked rapidly. "Oh," she said, one hand going to her heart. "No, sweetie, he's not dead. He's just been in an accident and I've been here the entire time, waiting to see if there was any chance that I could be with him so that he wasn't alone. I didn't know you were going to be here this quickly, but I promise you, I haven't left the hospital—"

Michelle held up a hand as she closed her eyes, clearly praying for patience. "Excuse me," she said, cutting off Elise for the second time. "I think you've been misled. I'm not Bradford's daughter."

The words hung in the air between them and Lucy felt her heart start to beat faster as she stood behind Elise, watching the scene unfold.

A slow, ice cold smile spread across Michelle's beautiful face. "As I said in my reply to your email, I'm his wife."

17

MARCH 21
ST. BARTS

The boat was manned by a quiet gentleman with a little mustache and a knowing smile.

"You like this spot?" he asked Finn and Carina, who looked at one another and then nodded enthusiastically.

The captain cut the engine and got everything settled before lifting a small door and then disappearing belowdecks.

"Wow," Carina said, looking over the side of the boat and breathing the salty air in deeply with a satisfied sigh. "I still can't believe you came to St. Barts alone, Finn."

He glanced around: blue sky, blue water, little chunks of land jutting into the sea as boats bobbed and people swam. Everyone was situated a safe distance apart as they ate, drank, and enjoyed the afternoon at Saline Beach, known for its nude swimming. It had seemed to Finn like a slightly naughty but terribly romantic place to bring the woman of his dreams.

"I came here alone because I needed something beautiful to take my mind off of the most beautiful thing I've ever known," he said, looking at her shoulder blades from behind as she held onto the railing of the boat and stared out at the horizon.

Carina turned to face him. "And did it work?"

Finn shook his head. "It absolutely did not work."

"It didn't work for me either," Carina said, keeping her eyes on his face. "I thought I knew what was best for us, and I was trying that whole 'it is better to have loved and lost than to have never loved at all' BS, but Finn..." She glanced around wildly, not making a move towards him. "I don't think I can live without you."

He watched and listened, adrenaline pumping through his veins as he took in the fact that the woman he loved with all his heart was here before him now, telling him that she felt the same. When her eyes finally landed on him, he reached out a hand and she took it. He pulled her close, resting his hands on her waist and feeling the warmth of her skin from beneath the thin dress she wore over her bikini. She was here, his Carina, within kissing distance. It wasn't just a dream.

Finn moved her even closer, so that their bodies pressed together and their lips were so close that they could feel each other's breath. As they stared into each other's eyes, their bodies continued to move, to sway slightly and reconfigure against one another, closing the distance—constantly closing the distance.

"I don't care what Shakespeare said," Finn whispered to her, reaching up and brushing a piece of hair from her cheek. "I don't want to love you and lose you—that's not better for me. I want to love you and keep you forever."

A small laugh escaped Carina's lips as she looked up at him, her arms wrapped around his neck. "My love," she said, smiling with adoration written plainly on her face, "I hope you didn't get an A in my class all those years ago, because that quote is actually from Tennyson, not Shakespeare."

Finn stopped swaying and his face fell theatrically. "Oh no," he said, shaking his head. "That's probably why I got a C."

Carina hugged him tighter and pressed her cheek to his chest. "I love you anyway," she said softly, closing her eyes.

"You love me even though I'm a kid who puts out fires and likes to be read to at night?"

Carina pulled back and looked at him, laughing again. "Finn!" she shouted playfully. "You're not a kid," she said, her face more serious. "And laying in bed with you as we read novels isn't childish, it's romantic. I'm crazy about you. I love you exactly as you are, with no reservations."

Finn stared at her face for as long as he could without saying anything, then finally, he spoke. "And I love you exactly as *you* are, with no reservations. So I'd like to ask you to never again think otherwise. I don't care about anything else but you. I don't mind if you have more wrinkles than me. It doesn't bother me that someday I might have to care for you—although we don't know that!" he added, pulling back to look at her squarely. "There are no guarantees. You might be the one caring for me."

"And I would," she said without hesitation.

"Just as I would for you."

"So," Carina said, taking a breath and composing herself. "Are we really doing this?"

"Baby, I've been really doing this all along. And there's nobody else I wanna do it with."

Carina's eyes sparkled with unshed tears as Finn slipped her cover-up over her shoulders, letting it fall to the wooden deck. He pulled his own shirt over his head with one hand and tossed it aside. They never broke eye contact as they finished taking off each piece of clothing, until finally, they were both naked. Carina glanced around self-consciously before Finn took her hand in his.

"Wow," he said, looking her up and down. "You're gorgeous." And before she could protest or make a joke to cover up her own insecurities, Finn bent forward to kiss her words away. "Let's go," he said, his lips still pressed to hers.

"Yeah?" Carina giggled like a girl. "You're ready?"

"I'm so ready." Finn stepped up to the edge of the boat, pulling her with him.

Together, fingers laced together with the solidarity of two soldiers heading into battle, they bathed for a moment in the warm sunlight, then counted down from three and jumped into the water together, squealing as the cold water touched every part of them, and laughing with joy because they were both braver than they ever knew they could be.

18

MARCH 21
ST. BARTS

Elise sat poolside at the hotel, looking stunned and as if she'd just been widowed for a second time. Even though the day was warm and balmy, she wore a thin blanket wrapped around her like a shawl, and a pair of large, black sunglasses shielded most of her face from view. For the first time since Lucy had met her, her red hair wasn't teased and sprayed into submission, but scraped back and clipped away from her make-up free face. This was not the Elise that Lucy had come to know and love.

"I guess it was too good to be true," Elise said stoically, holding a martini in one hand as she looked out into the distance with glazed eyes.

Lucy nodded but said nothing. This was uncharted territory for her, though she was no stranger to heartbreak and grief. Still, she'd never found herself head over heels for a married man, so it seemed wisest to keep her mouth shut and do the listening here.

"When Douglas passed away," Elise went on, pausing to sip her cold martini with two olives on a toothpick, "I swore to myself that I'd never love again and I haven't."

Again, Lucy just nodded. She'd ordered a sparkling water for herself because it seemed wisest not to go too far down the path of drinking every day starting at lunch, but she longed for a strong martini herself.

"I don't mean that I haven't been with men," Elise said unnecessarily, "I just mean I never loved any of them the way I loved my husband. He was a good man. A very good man."

Lucy's eyes focused on a woman in a sleek, striped turban that matched her swimsuit. Her toes and nails were short and glossy red, and her skin was the smoothest, most unblemished skin Lucy had ever seen. She sat beneath a palm tree, fanning herself with a magazine as she watched everyone on the pool deck with a bored look on her face. She looked like royalty from some exotic country.

Elise took a longer pull from her martini. She was starting to give off the distinct impression that she might just keep searching for the answer to her problems at the bottom of a glass.

"It sounds like you had a wonderful marriage," Lucy said, her eyes still on the woman in the turban. A waiter approached with a tray that held only a glass of ice and a diet Coke. The woman waved at the table near her and waited while the waiter poured the soda into the glass and set it down next to her. He walked away without being acknowledged in any way.

"Oh, I did," Elise said. "And I'd hoped that Bradford might be someone I could learn to love—if not as much, at least more than anyone else since Douglas—but in the end...I guess that's not meant to be." She suddenly turned to Lucy, snatched off her own sunglasses, and gave Lucy a hard look with her red-rimmed, mascara-free eyes. "I'm going to spend my life alone, aren't I?"

Lucy's mouth opened like she had something to say, but when she realized she didn't, she closed it again. She thought for a moment. "I guess there's the chance that we all might spend our lives alone," Lucy said after giving it some thought. "But we try, and that counts for something."

"What about you, Lucy?" Elise said in a raspy voice, raising a finger as a waiter passed to indicate that she'd like another martini.

"What about me?"

"You're here alone, but you've got a handsome friend with you. Is that a thing?" Elise drained her martini then fished out the toothpick and ate both olives with a flourish.

Lucy chewed on her bottom lip. "It could be," she said noncommittally. "We're good friends and we like each other. But life is never that easy, is it?"

The waiter swung by with a fresh martini for Elise. "Anything for you, miss?" he asked Lucy. She shook her head and mouthed "No, thank you" before he moved on.

"Why isn't it that easy?" This time Elise ate the olives first. Across the pool, the princess in the turban lifted her diet Coke and sipped it delicately through a straw as she crossed her perfect feet at the ankles. Men's heads turned her way like a row of dominoes collapsing.

"I guess because we're both about forty, and we've got lives and histories, and just like anyone, we're afraid. Or at least I am. I guess I shouldn't speak for Nick."

"Lucy!" Elise said too loudly, reaching over and slapping Lucy's thigh. "Don't be afraid of love. You're gorgeous, he's gorgeous, the sex would be amazing." Lucy's face went hot. "Ohhh, I see," Elise said, a knowing smile spreading across her face. "It *is* amazing. I see you, girl." She lifted a hand and wagged a finger at Lucy, giving her a semi-inebriated wink.

"Well, I've been married before and it ended badly," Lucy said. She spotted a loose thread on the hem of her shorts and tugged at it. "So I'm a little trigger-shy, you know? It's hard to put yourself out there fully when you've been burned."

"Amen to that." Elise lifted her glass and then took another drink. "I just got burned to a crisp. I'm like a side of bacon that someone left in the pan for too long." She hiccuped and her martini sloshed around in the glass. "I feel like I'll never be able to take the leap again. I thought Bradford was something real. I believed in him. Do you know how disappointing that is, Lucy?"

Did she know how disappointing it was to believe in someone and have them let you down? Her mind traveled back in time. Jason had come home from work one day looking troubled and apologetic.

Lucy had been cutting onions in the kitchen and sipping a glass of chardonnay as she waited for him, ready to use him as a sounding board and tell him all about the autopsy that she'd finished that day.

"Hey," Jason had said, dropping his messenger bag on the floor by the door. "We need to talk."

Lucy had stopped cutting and looked at him, and in that moment, she'd known that nothing would ever feel the same again.

"I do understand that disappointment," Lucy said now, meeting Elise's eye. "I was married for five years before my husband told me that he'd gotten a co-worker pregnant and that she was having the baby."

Elise's jaw dropped. "Honey," she said. "Honey, no."

Lucy pursed her lips and shrugged. "Yeah. We'd been trying for a baby ourselves—unsuccessfully, I might add—so it was honestly the most painful thing I could imagine happening at the time. It's still probably the most horrible end to a marriage that I could dream up."

Elise was staring at her, speechless, her martini held aloft but forgotten for a moment.

"Anyway," Lucy said. "Bad things happen. Life hurts. Love isn't always wonderful and it doesn't always end nicely. But we either go on after a heartbreak, or we don't. So are you going to go on?"

Elise pulled her wits about her and swirled the clear liquid around in her glass. The look on her face was far more like the old Elise than the new, stricken redhead that Lucy had walked up to just minutes earlier.

"I am," she said, giving a firm nod. "In time. But the real question here is, are *you* going to go on?"

Lucy's smile spread across her face as she reached for her sparkling water. "You know, I think I already am."

"Good for you, honey." Elise tossed back her drink and set the glass on the table with a drunken grin. "Good for you."

IT WAS PROBABLY TOO MUCH TO HOPE FOR, BUT LUCY AND ELISE HAD left the hospital together with very little drama after their interaction with Michelle and it had seemed as though the whole mess was behind them. The nurses had discreetly vanished from behind the desk to do their rounds or deliver medication, and Elise had wilted like a flower on the vine, nearly falling backwards into Lucy's arms after Michelle had announced who she really was. It had taken almost no convincing on Lucy's part to steer Elise through the corridors of the hospital and out into the bright sunlight, where she looked and acted stunned and confused. Lucy had gotten Elise back to the hotel and delivered her to her room for a shower without incident, and then they'd followed that up with their discussion at the pool.

But as Lucy stood in the middle of the lobby that evening consulting the list of people signed up to have cocktails at a bar with a view of the sunset followed by a night of dancing, she heard a loud discussion taking place at the front counter.

"I'm stunned. Absolutely *stunned* by the treatment I've received here."

"Ma'am, I am here to help you in any way that I can. Please allow me to buy you a drink at the bar and we can talk more—"

"Buy me a *drink*?"

Lucy was watching from her spot on the couch as Alvin tried unsuccessfully to calm Michelle Melton down. From the looks of it, Michelle was ready for battle. Lucy stood, unsure about whether she had any place in this discussion, though she was sure that because one of her travel guests was more than tangentially involved she could at least offer to help.

Before Lucy could approach the desk, Michelle set her expensive looking purse on the counter and spun around on her high heels, facing the entire lobby.

"Can I have your attention, please?" she asked loudly, clapping her hands together.

The man playing the piano tapered off, and the conversation

around the room went quiet. Everyone looked up from their drinks and their phones in anticipation.

"I'm just wondering," Michelle started, walking away from the front counter and towards the center of the lobby like a prosecutor making a point in a trial. "As a married woman who sent her husband on a trip to St. Barts so that he could compete in the regatta, should I have expected this fine establishment," she said, holding her arms wide and looking around the lobby, "to have encouraged my husband to carry on an affair with a *much* older woman?"

It was at this moment that Elise stepped off the elevator and into the middle of a real life drama. She stopped in her tracks, taking in the entire scene until her eyes finally landed on Lucy's stunned face.

"I'm not older than Bradford," Elise said lamely. "At least not more than a year or two, I don't think."

"*Honey*," Michelle said, feigning sweetness. "I meant you were much older than *me*. I can't even imagine what Bradford was thinking." She gave Elise a cursory once-over, making it clear by the disapproval written all over her face that she wasn't even worth that one glance.

Elise stood there, looking as small and as downtrodden as Lucy could imagine a woman looking. Her heart broke, but she didn't know what to do other than to go to Elise and put a protective arm around her, so that's what she did.

"We've got this," Lucy whispered in her ear, pulling her close. The soft, warm light of the chandelier shone on the top of the black lacquered piano, but the tuxedoed pianist sat there like everyone else, stilled by the spectacle before him.

Michelle took three long strides in Lucy and Elise's direction, stopping right smack in the middle of the lobby like an actor taking center stage.

"You are twice my age, darling," Michelle said, pointing a French manicured finger at Elise. "What were you thinking? That you'd snag a man of Bradford's status with your saggy body? Your Botoxed forehead? Your cheap perfume? You *reek* of desperation."

Elise held her breath.

"And this hotel had no problem just handing over a key to my husband's room, even though my name was on file."

The other guests were still watching, gobsmacked. A few people had started whispering, and Lucy noticed a teenage girl with her phone held up, undoubtedly taking video.

"He said you were his daughter," Elise said in a muted voice.

Michelle's chin dropped. "Are you blaming all this on Bradford? On a man who is basically in a coma, fighting for his life?"

Elise made a choking sound and Lucy tightened her grip on the older woman, hoping that her physical support would be enough to prop Elise up in the face of this debacle.

"He's in a coma?" Elise whispered, putting a hand to her mouth. "Poor Bradford."

"Poor Bradford is right," Michelle spat. "The man was here to compete in a boat race, not to be seduced by a gold-digging grandma." She turned back to Alvin with a gleam in her eye. "And you," she said to him. "You should probably consider contacting the wife if you have a man staying at your establishment who has fallen prey to this kind of nonsense." She swept a hand in Elise's direction. "If you see a clearly married man—and you knew he was because we've been here together on *more* than one occasion—you should consider intervening before he ruins his marriage. That's the job of a *true* concierge—someone who ensures the safety and happiness of all their guests."

Alvin had his hands clasped in front of him and his eyes were cast downward. He said nothing, though Lucy and every adult in the room knew that Michelle was clearly wrong: it was *not* the job of a concierge to keep track of his guests' extracurricular activities, and certainly not his job to call a wife to let her know that her husband was passing time with another woman.

Next to her, Lucy could feel Elise straightening and gathering steam. With a shrug of her shoulders, she let Lucy know that she didn't need her support anymore, so Lucy dropped her arm, watching to see what would happen next.

To the surprise of everyone in the lobby, Elise took two steps forward, nearly coming face-to-face with Michelle.

She cleared her throat. "First of all, your marriage is no one's business but yours, and it's also no one's job to police it. The concierge isn't responsible to let you know that your husband is tom-catting around, even with an old broad like me."

The teenager who was filming the scene looked on with wide eyes, tossing her silky hair over one shoulder as she glanced around at the faces of the adults to see if everyone else was as shocked by this gaudy display as she was.

"Secondly, Bradford represented himself as single, otherwise I never would have carried on with him. It's true that I'm lonely and I want to find someone to love, but I'm not desperate enough to take another woman's man. Even if he is married to a beautiful woman with a hideously ugly personality."

A titter passed through the lobby as the other women laughed appreciatively.

"And finally, you can keep your lying husband and his money. I'd never want to be with someone that terrible just for the material comforts. But if that works for you, then go for it. I hope Bradford ends up recovering, and I wish you both the best in life, but *honey*," she said, sarcastically echoing Michelle's use of the word, "between you and me and these four walls, he wasn't that good in bed anyway. So I hope he has *a lot* of money."

The titters turned to full-blown howls as women all around the lobby started to applaud, some getting to their feet like audience members at a talk show, ready to shout their support of a guest on stage. Lucy watched it all with barely concealed glee. Somehow, by dipping into a well of fortitude that she'd clearly possessed all along, Elise had found her footing again and put this ridiculous, preening, angry younger woman in her place. Lucy found herself clapping along with everyone else.

Michelle, however, was not amused. She strode back to the front counter, picked up the purse she'd left there, and kept walking—

straight through the front door and out to the portico, ostensibly to find a ride back to the hospital.

Within minutes, Elise was being sent drinks by some of the other guests, she'd gotten a high five from a woman who was clearly well into her 80s, and several people had stopped by to let her know that she'd done well putting Michelle in her place. A woman closer to Lucy's age had even leaned in and whispered to her while Elise was busy accepting a glass of champagne from a waiter, "He lied to me too." Before Lucy had a chance to process this and wonder whether maybe Bradford had been sleeping with multiple women on this same trip (the chances seemed good that he was), the woman drifted away, leaving Lucy to accept one of the drinks that was being sent to Elise.

She sipped it slowly, not wanting to be rude, but not wanting to drink too much before heading out for sunset cocktails. As she stood there, basking in the glow of Elise's moment in the spotlight, she smiled. Even though it wasn't her win, it was still a win for wronged women everywhere, and it felt good to watch Elise stand tall and straighten her crown.

But something nagged at Lucy as she smiled and nodded while other people circled, talking and laughing. Something felt off to her, and suddenly, as the piano player picked up again with a light, tinkling jazz number, she realized with a chill what it was: she knew what it felt like to be the injured party in a romance gone wrong, but she knew what it felt like to be in Michelle's shoes, too.

19

MARCH 23

ST. BARTS

The day was everything it should be: warm but not hot, sunny with wisps of white clouds floating through the sky, and just breezy enough to lift the chiffon of the bride's dress as she looked lovingly into the eyes of the man she was about to marry.

There, on the deck of the borrowed yacht, Carina stood facing Finn, her blonde hair swept into a loose knot at the nape of her neck, the bodice of a cream colored dress hugging her curves as she held a bouquet bursting with tropical flowers and greenery. Finn wore a suit and a smile so wide that he looked like he might vibrate right off the edge of the boat and into the water with the joy he was clearly holding inside.

As soon as Finn had come to her with his big news, Lucy had scrolled through her phone to find Eep, the man who'd invited her onto his yacht the night she'd gotten drunk and woken up married. He'd remembered her, of course, and been more than happy to let the little wedding party take place on his yacht before he left the following day. He'd even offered his catering crew to pitch in and told Lucy that he'd stay belowdecks while they danced and partied for a few hours after the ceremony, but she'd insisted he stay up top with everyone else. After all, the rest of the wedding guests were just fellow Holiday Adventure Clubbers, and Finn and Carina had insisted that they wanted it to be a happy, boisterous occasion.

"I feel a lot of love here," Eep said to Lucy, leaning over so that they were shoulder to shoulder. "I'm sure there's a big story with these two." He nodded at the bride and groom, who were posing for photos on the bow of the yacht, looking at one another with eyes full of wonder.

Lucy nodded, arms folded across her chest as she watched Carina and Finn. As they'd exchanged their vows, Lucy could feel her eyes filling with tears; happy occasions always did that to her. And maybe she'd felt a flicker of the hope she remembered from her own wedding day, felt that tangible joy that people experience as they promise to spend their lives woven together, attempting to make one another as happy as they can until the day they die.

"There's definitely a story there," Lucy agreed. "Just like every other couple." She smiled at Eep and bumped his shoulder with hers. "Thanks again for all of this," she looked around at the shiny deck with its long white bar, perfect bench seats, and tables laden with flowers and food. "I know you didn't have to do this for people who are total strangers to you, so I really appreciate it."

"You're no stranger, Lucy," he said, smiling at her and holding her gaze for a long beat. "And if you weren't here with a date, I'd ask you for a dance." Eep looked up just as Nick approached with two flutes of champagne. "Next time I'm in Florida, I'll look you up."

"Please do," Lucy said, and she meant it.

Eep gave Nick a nod and a smile as he moved away to check on the bar. He was as accomplished a host as Lucy had imagined he would be, and she really did owe him for this.

"Here you go, milady," Nick said, handing her the flute. They stood together for a moment, watching as Finn offered Carina his elbow. There was no denying their happiness or the fact that they were a stunning duo, and Lucy couldn't help but hope with all her might that they would make it for the long haul. Life was hard and other people could be cruel, but the warmth that emanated from this particular couple made her feel a spark of hope that she hadn't felt in a while. She wanted nothing more for them than a lifetime of togetherness, peace, and love.

When Finn had come to her with the request to help him make a wedding happen before they left St. Barts, Lucy knew that she had to give it her all. Not because Finn was a member of the tour group, but because she wanted to. Because she'd seen Elise go after the love she thought she wanted, and she'd watched her pick herself back up when she'd fallen. Because she'd seen Finn come on this trip alone to try and put the lost love of his life out of mind, and she'd been there as that great love reappeared to complete him. It all gave her hope: the good, the bad, the ugly, and the happily ever after, and she wanted to be a part of it all.

"Should we stroll?" Nick asked squinting in the bright afternoon light and offering Lucy his elbow just like Finn had done for Carina. Lucy slipped her arm through his and held her champagne in the other hand.

"I'd love to," she said, smiling up at him.

And that was one more reason why she'd wanted to pull this wedding together: because of Nick. Because he'd made her feel the promise of romance again. She had no idea where things would go once they were back home, but for the first time in a long time, she wanted to take the ride and find out.

20

APRIL 2

AMELIA ISLAND, FL

With only ten days to go until she stepped onto a plane for Edinburgh with the next tour group, Lucy was a blur of motion. Post-it notes with reminders were stuck to every surface of her life: her bathroom mirror, computer monitor, even the dashboard of her car. She'd come home from St. Barts on a high after her time with Nick, flown directly to Buffalo to check in with her mom and her aunt Sharon, spent three days arranging for more hands-on care, paying her mother's bills, and stocking the house with essentials, and then flown back to Florida to do some laundry and get on top of the details for this next adventure.

She was at her desk on a Thursday, answering emails from the next tour group when the door to her office flew open and a harried looking woman walked in.

"Hi, are you Lucy?" she asked, looking and sounding breathless.

Lucy stopped typing. "I am," she said. She stood up and came out from behind the desk. "How can I help you?"

"I'm Bailey Melton," the woman said, extending a hand for Lucy to shake. "Bradford Melton's daughter."

Lucy tried hard not to yank her hand away from Bailey's, but she was sure that her confusion was written all over her face.

"Don't panic," Bailey said, holding up both hands in surrender. "I come in peace."

"Okay," Lucy said, motioning for Bailey to sit in the chair across from hers. She sat down again behind her desk and waited to hear what Bailey had to say and why she was there.

"I'll just start by saying that Michelle is *not* my mother, which I'm sure is obvious, given that we're basically the same age."

"Right," Lucy said, nodding.

"My father has made some *choices*," Bailey said, with special emphasis on the word "choices." Her eyebrows lifted as she paused for a moment. "And I don't agree with all of them."

Lucy tilted her head to one side, considering the choices her own father had made—leaving her mother and effectively placing her care in Lucy's lap being the biggest one. She could probably relate to pretty much anything this woman was about to say.

"Anyhow," Bailey went on, "when I heard about what happened in St. Barts, I knew I needed to track you down and make things right. Oh," she said, waving a hand and shaking her head like she'd forgotten something important. "I should have mentioned that I live in Jacksonville, so this wasn't like a monumental trip or anything."

"Ah," Lucy said, lacing her fingers together on her stomach and leaning back in her chair. "Then you didn't fly in on a special mission or anything glamorous like that."

"No, no." Bailey laughed. She was truly a very pretty woman and she seemed kind, so Lucy tried to relax, certain now that Bailey wasn't there to continue Michelle's tirade or to say anything bizarre. "But my dad recovered from the accident and got to come home last week, and when I flew in to see him, he told me all about...the situation."

"I see," Lucy said, narrowing her eyes. She still had no idea where this was going.

"I'm not sure that you do," Bailey said, leaning forward and looking Lucy directly in the eye. "He's wanted to leave Michelle for years, and while I don't agree with his methods of moving on, or with the fact that he led some sweet woman to believe that Michelle was his daughter instead of his wife, I do agree with him finding someone nice and loving and who is far closer to his age than his current wife is."

Lucy took this in. It was relatable; she wasn't the biggest fan of the woman her dad had married after leaving her mother, but she wouldn't ever go so far as to drive forty-five minutes to deal with his messes after a vacation fling on a tropical island. If, in fact, that was what Bailey was there to do.

"Anyhow, he feels terrible about how things worked out with—is it Elise?"

"Yes, it's Elise," Lucy confirmed, looking at Bailey skeptically. "But did you really drive here to tell me this? Why doesn't your dad just let Elise know himself? I'm sure he has her number."

Bailey nodded as she pressed her lips together. "Well. That would be ideal, but my stepmother has him under lock and key at the moment, and the reason he can't just leave her is that they don't have a solid pre-nup. But that's a tale as old as time." She waved a hand again to indicate a subject change. "He did want to get something to Elise though, and I thought maybe if I came to you, you could forward it on to her. That way I'm not asking you to hand over any confidential information to me, and he's not getting more involved than he can or should be. Does that make sense?"

"I think so. You want me to mail something to Elise on Bradford's behalf?"

Bailey unzipped her purse and pulled out a folded white envelope. "If you would. I don't want to make a ton of work for you or anything, so I put it in a blank envelope and put the postage on it and everything." She thrust it in Lucy's direction.

Lucy stared at it for a second. "Can I ask what it is before I agree to send it? Purely because I don't want to upset Elise. She's a wonderful lady, and she doesn't deserve to have more reminders of what happened in St. Barts if it's just going to upset her."

Bailey nodded as she slipped the strap of her purse over her shoulder again. "Of course. I understand. It's a letter from my dad that I did not read, but that I understand is an apology of sorts, which I agree with him that she deserves. And I think he also included a check to reimburse her for the trip, because he feels that he ruined it."

Lucy took in a deep breath. "I don't want to confirm or deny that, since I'm not Elise, nor can I say whether she'll accept his money, but if it's truly an apology, I think I feel good about sending it. I'll put her address on it and get it into the mail this afternoon."

Bailey held onto her purse strap and gave Lucy a final nod. "Thank you so much. I really appreciate it, and I know my dad appreciates the chance to try and make things right. Sometimes it takes a person getting to a certain point in their lives before they're willing to make amends for the things they get wrong, you know?"

"I do know," Lucy said, holding up the envelope. "I'm on it."

"It was nice to meet you, Lucy." Bailey opened the door and then turned one last time before she walked out. "Cute place you got here." She gave Lucy a smile and then walked across the parking lot, opened the door to a silver Mercedes SUV, and got behind the wheel.

Lucy pulled up Elise's information on her computer and picked up a pen. *Would this be a welcome letter for Elise to receive? Should she warn her before she mailed it?* She wrote Elise's name and address in careful script and then stamped the upper left hand corner with the return address of The Holiday Adventure Club so that it wouldn't just get lost in the mail forever.

Next door, Nick had Elton John playing in the postal store and Hemingway was sprawled out near the p.o. boxes, as usual.

"Hey, hey," Nick said, tossing a stack of Express Mail envelopes on the counter and crossing the shop to greet her. "What brings you into my humble little place of business?"

Lucy stood up on tiptoes to put a kiss on his lips. "I need to mail something important."

"Oh?" Nick looked at her with open curiosity, still holding her by the waist after their quick kiss. "A letter to Santa Claus?"

Lucy rolled her eyes. "It's April, Nick. It's obviously a letter to the Easter Bunny."

He slapped his forehead. "Duh! Okay, let me get some postage on that for you ASAP."

"Actually, I just had a visit that will blow your hair back when you hear about it."

Nick was already halfway across the shop and about to pick up the discarded Express Mail envelopes when he turned to look at her. "Spill the beans, girl. I'm ready."

"Remember Bradford Melton?"

"Douchebag Extraordinaire? Yes, I definitely remember him." Nick stacked up the envelopes as they talked, tapping their edges against the front counter to make a neat pile that he could shelve in a cubby for customers to access them.

"His daughter just drove in from Jacksonville to deliver a letter— and, she says, a check—for me to mail to Elise."

Nick looked puzzled. "A check? To what—say he's sorry with money?"

"Apparently. Although his daughter said it was more like he wanted to pay for Elise's vacation since he ruined it."

"He sure as hell did," Nick said, looking angry on Elise's behalf. "Guys like that..."

"I know, I know," Lucy said, holding up the envelope. "But I think it's the right thing to do, sending it. And I'll send her a quick email and let her know it's coming so she's not surprised."

"Well, if you think it's best to send it, then you gotta do what you gotta do." Nick nodded at the mail slot.

With the envelope held aloft like a magician showing the audience that no sleight of hand was taking place, Lucy walked over and slipped it into the opening. "There. It's out of my hands now. Let the universe take over."

Nick finished putting his envelopes away and walked back over to Lucy, putting his hands on her waist again. "The universe *can* be a pretty magical place," he said, lowering his lips to hers again. "It's done some great things for me lately."

"Oh yeah?" Lucy laughed, kissing him back. "What do you think it'll do next?"

Nick looked out the window thoughtfully, pulling her even closer.

"Hopefully the universe will tell you that you should have dinner with me tonight."

"Dinner? That's all you want?" She smiled at him, feeling a happiness like she hadn't known in a long, long time.

"I'm a simple man." Nick shrugged.

"Hey, I'm a simple girl," Lucy said, running her hands up his arms and wrapping them around his neck. "And it just so happens that dinner is my favorite meal."

"So it's a date?"

"Nick Epperson," she said, feeling warm and woozy in his arms. "It's a date."

READY FOR THE NEXT BOOK IN THE HOLIDAY ADVENTURE CLUB SERIES?

Join the Holiday Adventure Club as they take a trip to Scotland for Easter. Buy it today from your favorite bookstore here!

ABOUT THE AUTHOR

Stephanie Taylor is a high-school teacher who loves sushi, "The Golden Girls," Depeche Mode, orchids, and coffee. She is the author of the *Christmas Key* books, a romantic comedy series about a fictional island off the coast of Florida, as well as *The Holiday Adventure Club* series.

https://redbirdsandrabbits.com
redbirdsandrabbits@gmail.com

ALSO BY STEPHANIE TAYLOR

Stephanie also writes a long-running romantic comedy series set on a fictional key off the coast of Florida. Christmas Key is a magical place that's decorated for the holidays all year round, and you'll instantly fall in love with the island and its locals.

To see a complete list of the Christmas Key series along with all of Stephanie's other books, please visit:

Stephanie Taylor's Books

To hear about any new releases, sign up here and you'll be the first to know!